RED MORNING CHILD

To -
Brianna
Hope you Enjoy!

MICHAEL ASSELIN

Michael Asselin

If you would like to know about new releases and upcoming
adventures, please sign up for my mailing list at: http://
eepurl.com/dPVw8H

Edited by: Editing for Authors
Cover designed by: Covers by Christian
Map Drawn by: Michael Asselin

THE NORTH WOODS WILDS

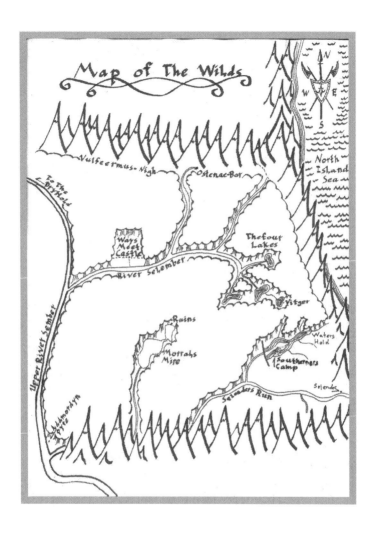

CHAPTER ONE

In the dark Kritcha waited. Listening. The air almost perfectly still except for her ragged breath. The pounding of her own heart that in the unnatural stillness of the night sounded like the beating of great fists upon the earth. The ground tasted wrong. It was cold and bitter like dead things left to rot. Kritcha's bare feet soaked up the taste of the earth better than her ears could hear or her eyes could see. Tonight every sense told her something was wrong.

Kritcha moved forward. Keeping to the shadows. Flitting from tree to tree like a shadow herself, careful not to disturb the unnerving silence.

The houses were dark. No light shone from any of the windows. She was certain all the world could hear the dull booming beats of her heart as she crouched under the window of a darkened house. But on this night she didn't care about the rest of the world, only those things that came from the lakes. She shivered and moved from below the window. Rounding a corner, she saw the length of the village.

A narrow dirt track ran up the middle. Small stone houses crowded along it. There were only about seven of them. Thatched roofs slick with a summer's rain glowed in the light of the night's three moons: one half and two quarters.

Kritcha turned away, leaning back against the moist stones of the house and took a deep breath. Wondering to herself if they could already hear her heartbeat. Could already sense the warmth of her blood. Could already taste it on their cold lips and feel it filling their wretched bellies.

She took another deep breath. The pounding of her heart slowed for a moment, and she heard something, a distant sound like the patter of bare feet on muddy earth. And she knew it was them; it could only be them. The people of the village did not go barefoot as she did. Only *they* did.

She turned and looked again. Now there was a glow coming from the window of a house at the far end of the village. It was little more than a flicker. The small light of a single candle. Lit especially for her.

The old couple were still alive then. Maybe the Laroo weren't here tonight. Maybe she had worried over nothing, had made it all up, but the ground tasted so strange. So dead. So cold.

She shuddered again and moved silently through

the village. Stopping at the end of every house, looking in every window. As she drew closer she slowed her pace. Her heart thundered in her ears as she strained to listen for the sound of more footsteps in the mud. Kritcha drew a hatchet from the folds of her deerskin jerkin.

Her eyes moved back to the flame in the window now so close to her, but there was something strange about the flame. It didn't flicker and dance the way candles normally did. This seemed constant and solid. She realized to her horror that it was growing rapidly.

Kritcha ran forward, her hatchet raised, gripping it tightly in her sweating palm. And she knew too late the error of her haste. From all around her hisses issued from the darkness.

Low guttural utterances she had heard so many times before, in her nightmares. And she could hear them all about her, the soft patter of webbed feet on mud. The click of nails on the stones of the houses. Nails as long as fingers and nearly as dexterous.

Kritcha froze. Unable even to breathe waiting for the inevitable pinch of the sharp nails penetrating her flesh. They hesitated, grotesque bodies poised, waiting in the darkness just out of her sight. The shadows shielding them from her eyes and the light of the growing fire set alight before them.

They started to call. From the dark their odious voices rose in unison, like a great and terrible chorus.

Gitcha, Gitcha, Gitcha, Gitcha. It seemed to come from everywhere at once.

Gitcha, Gitcha, Gitcha, Gitcha. A horrible croaking bellow from deep in their frog throats, they called out again and again. The awful sound filled her ears. She closed her eyes. The ground tasted like blood.

And she was in another place. Another time. She could smell the fire again just like the blaze before her now. Feel its heat. It was the same as her nightmares. This place now, the fire in front of her and the time before, when she was younger. When she was weaker.

She opened her eyes and could still hear those screams. The screams of her youth, the screams in her nightmares. Those guttural calls in the dark.

Gitcha, Gitcha, Gitcha, Gitcha.

She could see them now, black bulbous eyes reflecting the firelight. Rounded heads turning back and forth looking from one to another and then back to her and then the fire. Rows of fine razor-sharp teeth shone out each time they croaked. Some clicked their nails together. Others on the stones of the houses. They were drawing nearer now.

Kritcha closed her eyes again, taking a long, deep breath as she did. She began a slow exhale but was interrupted as the door of the house in front of her burst open in a shower of splinters and sparks.

Quickly she opened her eyes and broke from her trance, poised and ready to strike at whatever should venture forth from the inferno beyond the door.

4

It was a Gitcha-a-Laroo. One bigger than any she had ever seen. Instead of ambling slowly in a crouched stance like the rest, it stood upright. So tall was the thing that it had to incline its head to look down at her.

In its claws it held a figure. As the Laroo's eyes wandered over Kritcha from its gaping maw came a great bellowing chortle. So great that it silenced the other Laroos' own chorus.

Then the brute cocked its head back. Turning its eyes from Kritcha to the moonlit sky. As it did the great Laroo puffed out its throat and bellowed so loudly that Kritcha felt it even over the pounding of her own heart.

The figure held in the Laroo's claws shook and raised its head. It looked around, eyes peeled wide, glowing in the darkness cast by the brute that held it. Kritcha could not see features on the face itself, but she could see the beard. She could see it, normally neat and adorned with trinkets that had been flung loose in the violence of the night. It was him. It was her friend. Her teacher. Calleh.

Where was his wife? Where was Semila? Dead. Kritcha had no doubt, already the feast of the Laroo. Her warm blood in their bellies. Kritcha cringed ever so slightly at the thought.

The bellowing ceased. The great brute holding her teacher looked down at Kritcha. Its frog lips twisted. Curling this way and that. It looked as though it might spit a bad taste from its mouth, but before it could, Kritcha called out to her friend,

"Calleh!"

Eyes wide with terror focused on her.

"Kritcha!" he said. He choked, coughing from the smoke.

"Kritcha—" he coughed again.

"Calleh!"

She wanted to run to him, but she remembered all the other Laroo waiting in the shadows. She raised her hatchet and tightened her grip. She took one step, and the other Laroo resumed their awful chorus.

Gitcha, Gitcha, Gitcha, Gitcha-a-Laroo!

She took another step. Her eyes fixed on the big Laroo. Its lips still moving like it was going to spit.

"No, Kritcha!" Calleh convulsed in a fit of coughing.

She looked down from the Laroo's eyes and into Calleh's.

"Run, Kritcha!"

His chest exploded outward as a great clawed hand thrust through it.

"No! Calleh!"

Kritcha rushed forward. Her mind focused on the hand and her friend. Forgetting the croaking mass about her. The hand retracted, and Calleh fell to the ground. She followed her old friend to the ground, and with blood frothing upon his lips he gasped out to her,

"Green Boughs—"

"What?" she asked, desperate.

"Remember—"

"Calleh!"

"Boughs."

His head fell limp to one side. Kritcha looked up to see the bulbous frog eyes glowing in the fire light. The big one above her, its mouth still working, eyes still staring.

It opened its mouth. Short needle teeth a sickening yellow. Its lips still moved as though they were struggling to find the right contortion to make words.

It leaned closer still, and Kritcha could smell it even over the smoke of the blaze behind it. The smell of swamp and rot and mold. The smell that made her cringe even in broad daylight. The smell that she smelled in her dreams when she woke sweating and screaming.

"Warm ones, warm ones, good blood, good blood, yum, yum. Taste the blood warm one, you'll like it too."

It was speaking to her. The big brute was speaking.

"Cold blood, cold skin. Warm blood, warm flesh. Soft and supple it all cuts the same!"

Kritcha moved as fast as she could. Her right hand moved from her hatchet and pulled a short knife from her jerkin. She threw it at the big Laroo and swung her hatchet behind her with her left, catching the Laroo she knew had to be coming. Her knife met its eye, and the thing howled. The others paused to hear the big one's cry.

Kritcha plunged forward into the thick of the frogs. Their cold blood covered her face and body as she

7

hacked her way through them. She heard the big Laroo's voice behind her.

"Warm one, warm one, Kritcha."

She shuddered but couldn't stop. She was at the edge. Almost free. She was faster than them on land. Much faster.

As she ran, the soft patter of their feet grew quieter, but the bellows of the big Laroo seemed to get louder.

"Warm one, warm one, Kritcha!"

Kritcha ran as hard as she could to the nearest tree she could scale. The Laroo couldn't climb.

Gitcha, Gitcha, Gitcha, Kritcha, Gitcha-Kritcha, Gitcha-a-Larooooo!

From branch to branch she ran dodging like a squirrel harried by a hound. Their chant still echoed.

Gitcha-Kritcha, Gitcha-Kritcha, Gitcha-Kritcha, Gitcha-a-Larooooo!

CHAPTER TWO

A plume of blue-gray smoke rose to the north. Had the Laroo attacked again? Had they burned another village in the night? Sten watched in silence. Two nights in a row. They were getting closer. Sweat beaded on his brow. Already it ran into his eyes. The sun had not yet risen above the mountains. The day would be unbearably hot.

From behind him, the crunch of dried grass caused him to turn. Two soldiers, neither wearing more than rough canvas shirts and leather trousers. Sweat ran down their faces. Mud and soot covered their torn clothes.

"What did you find, Sergeant?" asked Sten.

"The villagers were already dead when we got there," said the soldier on the right, whom Sten noted had a face that one might be lucky for even a mother to love. It looked as though he had eaten an overly sour apple and his face had frozen, permanently, into that grimace.

"The Hoppers burned the village," said the soldier on the left. He had the unfortunate malady to appear as though his mother had dropped him when he was very young, flattening his face, which also seemed unusually round, not unlike a pancake.

"Did you find any alive?"

"Only one was still alive," said the pancake-faced soldier.

"Where is it?" asked Sten.

"We got it over in one of the tents staked down nice and deep, tied and chained and everything. They must have thought it was dead too," replied the pancake-ish soldier. "Brutes just left it there with the two dead ones, it put up one 'ell of a fight too. Once it woke up."

"Don't even take their dead," said the sour-faced soldier.

"Did you?"

"Did we what?" they asked together.

"Take their dead?" Sten asked getting a little impatient.

"We did. Added them to the pile this morning," said the sour apple.

They were starting to get quite a collection of Hopper bodies now. The smell was almost unbearable.

Sten nodded, "Show me the tent; I want to see this one. I want to see what it knows."

Both soldiers hesitated and glanced at each other.

"Yes, *sir*." They both responded in almost perfect unison.

"This way," said the pancake.

"Did they follow you?"

He shook his head.

Sten followed the two soldiers, who were sweating worse than he was, back towards the camp. Canvas and cloth tents covered almost half the peninsula. Three separate camps had been erected in the last two weeks. Each overlooked the reservoir, one on the east bank, one on the west. The third sat at the northern tip of the peninsula. The reservoir was the only safe place from the Hoppers. The bottom was barren and hard, devoid of all the mud the Hoppers loved so much to hide in.

The three entered a tent. The interior was dark, almost black despite the light of the rising sun. A sickening odor of swamp and rot poured over the three as they entered. The two guards stationed to watch ran out as they entered, almost knocking over the two with Sten. He turned and watched as the two guards vomited on the ground just outside the tent. The two with him looked nervously at each other. He pushed forward.

The Hopper was asleep. Or passed out. Sten couldn't be sure. He didn't care.

Sten knelt, leaning toward the creature. With his face close to the Hopper's the stench was overwhelming. But Sten had smelled it before; he was used to it. Its lips curled back away from pointed teeth. Sten

11

looked over the body. Blood still ran slowly from a wound in its chest.

"Who did this?" Sten asked as he poked at the wound.

"We don't know."

"What?" Sten turned from the creature.

"We found it like this, Sir," said the pancake-faced soldier.

"The rest were dead, Sir."

Sten nodded slowly, and turned back to the creature.

"Someone did this. How many human bodies did you find?"

"The remains of twenty-five were found, Sir," said the pancake. The sour apple was quiet; Sten turned and glanced up at him. Even in the dark of the tent Sten could see that his face was flush; maybe he would puke too.

"How many villagers were there a week ago when you visited them?"

"Twenty-five, Sir."

"So someone else did this. Someone who might still be alive."

"How do you know it wasn't one of the villagers?"

"Because I've seen when the Hoppers attack." Sten stood.

"They come in the night. Usually warm summer nights like the ones we've been having lately. They slip silently from the water. Their webbed feet make no noise. Except when they want them too. When fear and the knowledge of their approach can serve them. Their long nails break locks or pull shutters from windows, and before anyone can move the entire village is dead." Sten turned to the soldiers.

"The bodies were still in the houses, weren't they?"

"All but one."

"Where was that one?"

"It was charred and burnt like the rest..." the soldier paused, "but..."

"What?"

"It wasn't stripped clean like the rest," said the pancake, "Like it wasn't eaten."

The sour-faced soldier nodded and looked like he would hurl his breakfast at any second.

"The rest were just bones." The sour-faced soldier winced and swallowed hard, as though speaking had almost let the breakfast he was so desperately trying to keep, go free. "This one still had skin and muscles. Organs too." He finished once he had regained some control.

"They needed that person for something."

"Needed it?" asked the pancake-faced soldier.

"They wanted it for some other purpose." Sten looked down at the creature.

"But I thought they were just stupid Hoppers. Mindless brutes that only kill and eat."

Sten shook his head without looking away from the creature.

"Those are stories. Maybe the ones your mother used to tell you to scare you if you were lucky enough to have a mother to care so much. These creatures are brutes." Sten prodded a bound leg with the toe of his boot.

"But they are certainly not mindless. They are as crafty as they are slippery and twice as vicious as a bear when trapped in a corner." Sten raised the sleeve of his right arm revealing a long, jagged scar that ran up past his elbow and disappeared under his sleeve.

"This is from one of their southern cousins." He rolled the sleeve back down.

"Is that how you lost your fingers too?" asked pancake-face.

Sten looked down at his hands. Pausing for a moment to consider how he had lost those fingers. Three from his left, leaving just thumb and index. Two from his right, leaving thumb, middle, and little finger. His constant reminder of the trap he had misjudged. Of the trap that had almost cost him his life.

"No," Sten said, rubbing the gaps where his fingers had been.

He looked back at the Hopper whose silent form still sat hunched against the stake to which it was tied.

"I've been hunting these things for ten season turns under the order of the Queen of White Lilies. There aren't many left down south, but up here—" he looked back at the soldiers first left then right.

"Wake it up."

14

The soldiers glanced at one another; both wanted to be free from the stench. Neither wanted the thing to wake up.

"Wake it up." Sten's voice was low, but there was no anger. He understood their reluctance, but he needed to find whoever had stabbed the Hopper and killed the two others.

A pail of water was produced. Sten dipped his hand in. Frigid. The spring water was ice cold. Drawn fresh that morning from the stream before it met with the much warmer waters of the reservoir.

He took the pail and emptied it on the head of the Hopper. For a second there was nothing, save a hushed silence and the chortle of cicadas.

It coughed and spit up blood and bile. The two soldiers stepped back. Sten leaned closer.

The teeth snapped into a snarl that met only inches from Sten's face. The Hopper twisted and writhed to be free from the ropes that held it to the stakes driven deep into the ground.

"Warm blood! Warm blood!" It spat at Sten. Its blood and spit covering his face.

The soldiers moved back another step. Both almost to the entrance of the tent. Their swords drawn.

The thing's eyes lolled back and forth switching from the soldiers to Sten and back and forth and back again.

"Warm blood! Warm one! Warm blood!"

"What have you been doing out there at night?

What are you looking for?"

"Warm one! Warm one!"

"Why have you come so far south?" Sten asked the creature.

"Warm blood! Warm blood"

Sten grabbed it by the throat. With one hand he pushed its head away from his own. It fell back landing on one of the stakes to which it was bound, letting out a piercing howl. Its jaws snapped, and its teeth clicked. Bound hands shook and jerked. Helpless claws twisted to be free.

"Why are you moving south?"

"Warm one. Warm blood. Cousins, Cousins. Green Boughs!"

Sten turned to the soldiers. "We have to go to the village. Take me there now."

The soldiers looked at one another and then at the Hopper, still writhing.

"Now!"

"Yes, Sir." They both sheathed their swords and backed from the tent. Their eyes never left the Hopper.

"You want what?" the old commander asked.

"I need—" started Sten.

"I know what you said, huntsman. I may be old, but I'm neither deaf nor a fool. The answer is no. You will not take my soldiers out to die. I don't care who you are or what you've done to impress the White Lily, you've seen what those things are. Up here..."

"I've seen what they are. I've hunted them for—"

Commander Crittondone shook his head.

"You want twenty soldiers? How about you go out there yourself? How about you go out there and get yourself killed, and then I won't have to deal with you anymore? How about that, huntsman?"

Commander Crittondone turned away from Sten.

"And what when she hears of my death? The White Lily won't—"

The old commander laughed.

"What? What will she say? Will she call you a fool? A blithering idiot? I don't care what she'll say. You're not a soldier, and I won't allow you to lead soldiers. If you want to go off and die, then be my guest, but don't take any more to die with you."

Sten started to speak but thought better of it. He made to leave but was stopped by the old commander's gruff voice.

"Get your sorry carcass from my camp. Go out and hunt the Hoppers or Laroo or whatever you call them. Maybe I'll see you again when the Hoppers wear your hide like you wear the White Lily's favor."

Sten clenched his teeth and left the sweltering heat of the tent for the abysmal heat of the morning sun. He returned to his own tent. Gathering up what small supplies he needed, he made ready to venture north beyond the reservoir to find the village.

The two soldiers were still guarding the Hopper's tent. Both watched him uneasily as he passed. The cowards wouldn't even go back inside. He could still hear the creature as he passed, snapping and snarling. Sten wondered how long it could go on like that. He wondered if the northern Hoppers were as protective of their colonies as their southern cousins. They might want to watch the water that night. Even the water of the reservoir might not be as safe as they thought. Just because Hoppers didn't usually go in them didn't mean they wouldn't dare for one of their own.

Sten walked out from the palisade erected at the base of the peninsula. He skirted the edges of the enormous reservoir heading north to where he thought the village was. There were still some scant traces of the smoke from their fires in the air. That gave him something at least.

Sten walked until mid-afternoon, when the sun was highest and the day hottest. He stopped at a small rocky stream. The water moved slowly, and he bent to gather some for a drink and to rinse his face. He paused for a moment, the hazel eyes, his mother's eyes, regarded him calmly from the surface of the stream. Those were eyes he hadn't seen in a very long time. Those were eyes he didn't miss.

He hadn't seen her in maybe twenty seasons' turns. Maybe it was more; the seasons came and went so quickly. He had only seen nine, maybe ten turns then, when she had gone, when she had left him alone. The face that looked back at him was tired, worn and weary with the journey north. Long black hair held back from his face with a leather thong, tied neatly behind his head. His tanned skin flushed red with the morning's trek.

He cupped his hands, scooping the wonderfully cold water into them. The water was frigid. It chilled him, and he felt refreshed. He sat on a rock and chewed thoughtfully on a green apple.

Three questions had bothered him all morning and afternoon as he had walked. Why had the Hoppers come so far south, and what had it meant by Green Boughs? What was so important to them that they left three of their fallen behind? The southern Hoppers never left their dead or wounded. Usually the northern breed of the Hoppers did not go near the man-made waters of the reservoir. Something about them the Hoppers didn't like. But they were closer now. Why?

Sten took another bite. As he did, he noticed a flash in the trees. It was something big. But it was strange, almost like a squirrel. He stood, taking one last bite of the bitter apple, and tucked the core in his pack. He moved silently in the direction of the mysterious shape in the trees. He caught a glimpse again. It was moving quickly. Very quickly. Sten made to chase it. Maybe whatever it was knew what had happened in the village. Maybe it could tell him what the Hopper would not.

CHAPTER THREE

K ritcha sat. Listening. Back against the trunk of an ancient oak tree. Her feet dangled in the air, her legs straddling a thick branch. Sweat poured in thick rivulets down her face and back. Her thin deer-hide shirt clung to her body. She took several deep breaths to slow her heart. She had not stopped running. Only lessened her pace after a while. For the entire night and most of the morning she had kept it up. Even when her legs had been too weak, even when her lungs felt like they were on fire. She had kept going. She didn't know where in her desperation she had gone. Or how far she had actually come in the dark. For the first time she felt pain in her sides and on her face. Blood soaked her clothes as well as sweat. Her shirt, sliced in several places where the claws of the Laroo had grabbed at her. Scratches covered her hands and face from where the branches had whipped her in the dark.

She closed her eyes. She let the gentle swaying of the tree lull her to sleep. She should be safe. The Laroo were too slow. They would never have come this far. It had been a day and a night since she had last seen them; she should have put them far behind her by now. Yet she couldn't shake a fear that clung to her like sweat. That they knew where she had gone. That they had kept up their pursuit and that even now they were closing in about her.

Just as she began to drift off, she heard a snap. Her tired body was on alert in an instant. Tensed like a spring she listened, ready to shoot up and vanish, despite her exhaustion. More snaps. The movement of many feet. Clumsy feet. Feet not accustomed to the forest. Laroo feet.

She began to climb, careful not to make a sound. Her eyes widened, and her ears strained to catch any sign that they had spotted her. She looked around her. Hidden in the canopy she felt at least a little better. There was nothing now. No sticks being broken. No leaves being crushed under careless feet. Had they stopped?

Her heart slowed to a normal pace once again. As it did, her eyelids began to droop. Heavy with the effort of fearful flight. She shook her head, straining to remain vigilant. Again her head began to fall when she heard another snap. She waited, listening for more. Had they stopped? Had they caught sight of her?

Slinking down one branch lower, she scanned the forest trying to pierce the dense green fog of foliage that surrounded her. The forest about her filled with all manner of sounds. Birds fluttered around her, moving from branch to branch. Squirrels too played at chase in the branches near her. But they began to chatter, aware of the danger that was approaching.

Peering out through the forest, Kritcha feared what she would see. The shambling hop of a mass of frogs. Her fear made all the worse for their silence. Why did they not call out like they normally did? There was more crunching of leaves and the careless snap of fallen branches. They were getting very close. Yet she didn't run. For some reason her curiosity held her there, and she, along with the birds and squirrels, waited. They listened and waited for those that disturbed the peace of their forest.

She caught it, but only briefly, a flash of black through the green and brown of the forest. The careless feet were moving closer to her perch. Kritcha moved around the tree, putting the massive trunk between her and the black shape below.

Watching with her face half hidden behind the trunk, she saw them now. A group of men. There were at least ten of them. Most wore black leather armor, others brown. They all carried swords and rough packs slung over their shoulders. They were soldiers. Kritcha had seen more like them before. The way they stayed together so neat and orderly. The way they carried themselves, watching, but paying little heed to the forest about them. Southerners. They had dark hair but pale skin. So not too far south. But what were southern soldiers doing so near the waters' hold? Venturing north of it no less.

Kritcha kept her distance but followed them the rest of the afternoon. They stopped near a small muddy stream, one that didn't flow straight into the reservoir. They moved about setting their camp for the night. As Kritcha watched them, her eyelids again began to fall to the heavy pressure of exhaustion. She tried to fight. Tried to resist. She had been fighting too long. It was a fight she couldn't win. Not anymore.

Kritcha jumped. With a start, she was awake. She peered into the darkness about her. The fire the soldiers had built dwindled and was little more than a glow now. Kritcha stood on the branch, crouched, ready to move in an instant. What had roused her from her slumber? What had caused her to jump?

She listened. Waiting for any sound. For any indication of what might be waiting for her in the dark. There was a rustle of leaves from below, and she sprang upward, reaching for the next branch. Her reach fell well short of the branch above. Something held her back. Something gripped her about the ankle and held fast. As she leaped up, it held her, and with a rough jerk she was pulled back down. It was only a moment that she stopped, hardly long enough for her realize what was going to happen next. She swung around a lower branch, her head narrowly missing the branch she had leapt from. Two more revolutions and she slowed, hanging there, her tether wrapped about a branch. Leaving her to dangle, helpless in the dark.

"Who are you?" asked a voice from the dark.

Kritcha didn't answer. She strained her eyes to see the source. Even in the light of three sister moons she couldn't see a face or even a figure for that matter.

"Why were you following these soldiers?" asked the voice. Still Kritcha could not see the source.

"I was curious," she replied.

"About what?" asked the voice.

"Why southern soldiers are wandering so haplessly through my forest." She twisted against the bond that held her aloft. It was cutting off circulation to her foot, and her left hip felt as though it might be out of its place.

"Your forest?" asked the voice from below. It sounded closer now, if only slightly.

"Well, it's certainly not theirs."

Krticha tried harder to be free.

"Who are you?" it asked.

"I'm nothing. I'm no one."

"A nothing the Hoppers left alive; a no one that they set a trap for. Why would they do that?" the figure paused, maybe to give her a moment to think, "For a *nothing*."

His emphasis on the last word made her shudder. It was a question she had asked herself, but she hadn't had much time to think it over. She had spent all of her waking hours running for her life.

"I don't know why they would've set a trap for me. All I know is that they did, all I know is that they held my friend and murdered an entire village to get me, so maybe you're right. Maybe I am more than just nothing to someone. But I am, it seems, slipperier than their claws can manage on land."

She would have cut the bonds had she not left her tools behind in her flight from the Laroo.

A figure cast in moonlight materialized out of black shadows.

"If you want to go free, tell me who you are. Tell me where you come from. Maybe I can help you." The figure moved closer to her.

"Why would you want to help me? I don't even know who or what you are, and for that matter you don't know who I am."

In the three moons' light, she saw the figure pull something from a sheath. The sparkle of well-honed steel flickered in her eyes and she writhed all the more against her tether.

"I am a hunter. I've come up here to find out why the Hoppers have been moving south, and if you play into this then our purpose would be the same. You want to know why they singled you out? You want to know why they killed an entire village? Your friend?"

said the figure. Now he stood below her, his face pale and stern in the white glow of the sister moons.

Kritcha was beginning to feel dizzy. Already the swinging and the blood in her head were taking over. The figure below was blurry now. Where there had been hard moonlit lines now there were spots of burning light. She closed her eyes.

"I will find out who you are one way or another," the figure growled.

"Green... boughs..." was all that she managed to say. She opened her eyes again and could swear that for a second the figure had a look of shock on his face. Then there was nothing. She felt only falling.

It was screaming. It was the smell of a horrid swamp. The taste of blood. And she was awake again. Up like a bolt but her head swam as though she were still dangling from the branch.

"Crittondone would not send you with me, but he'll send you out on your own to blunder haplessly through the woods," said a voice. It sounded to Kritcha like the one who had spoken to her while she had been hanging from the tree, but she couldn't be sure. Her head was still spinning.

"Do you know how long she was following you?" asked the voice. The hunter, she guessed.

"We didn't know she was following us at all," said another voice. One of the soldiers, Kritcha thought.

"And you were supposed to be following me. What exactly were you doing?" said the hunter.

"Trying to get back to the village," said another soldier.

"S'where we thought we'd find you, Sir," said another.

"You should be more careful. She was following you the entire day," said the hunter.

"How do you know that?" asked one of the soldiers.

"Because I was following her the entire day."

Kritcha tried to sit up. Her head swam. Her hands and feet were bound. They hadn't noticed her attempt to sit up. She closed her eyes and lied back down.

"You say that you were going to the village?"

"Yes, Sir," said one of the soldiers. All of their voices sounded so similar.

"Then why were you going this way? Couldn't you see the smoke?" the hunter asked.

"What'd you mean, *Sir*?" asked one of the soldiers.

"I mean that the direction you're heading is not toward the village. I mean that you have no idea what you're doing out here. You built a fire. Do you have any idea how much the Hoppers like the warmth of a fire?"

There was no immediate response from the soldiers. Kritcha wondered, *Hoppers*? He must mean the Laroo. And she hadn't thought about it, but yes, the fools had built a fire. And a muddy stream. Had they really come that far from the waters' hold? She strained to listen. To hear what other sounds the night held. She heard nothing.

She wiggled and twisted against her bonds. Pulling

at her wrists and ankles to be free from the ropes. The soldiers turned to look at her, watching her fruitless struggle.

"How stupid are you?" she cried through gasps of panicked breath.

"Let me—" Then she heard it. Soft and wet. A foot in mud. A careful foot. A foot that carried a grotesque body with cruel intention. Then she heard another and another.

The soldiers' eyes followed hers to the banks of the stream. Where in the pale light of the moons something was moving. Very slowly it rose from the stream. A shadow glistening wet in the night. *Gitcha-Gitcha, Gitcha-Gitcha.*

Kritcha rolled over and sat upright, the fog of her unconsciousness obliterated by the fear that overwhelmed her. She tried to work her hands free to get her feet unbound, but it was no use. She worked her hands to her front and rolling back onto her stomach she pushed herself up. It was just as she was almost standing that the blow came. It was piercing. Like a knife in her side. But it wasn't a knife she knew. It was a long claw, like a finger that wormed its way inside of her, tearing her skin open.

A voice in her ear whispered with a foul breath of swamp.

"Warm one. Warm blood." It licked its lips.

"Warm flesh. Warm blood. *Gitcha-Kritcha, Gitcha-Kritcha.*"

The claw retracted from her flesh. She tried to stay awake. To fight through the pain. But it was too much. She needed rest. She needed sleep. And as she fell, the distant words of cruel lips filled her ears.

"Warm ones, Warm bloods. Green Boughs! Green Boughs!"

CHAPTER FOUR

Kritcha walked as best she could. Her feet moved but not of her own will. Prodded along by vicious hands that stabbed her with jagged claws, she stumbled blindly forward. At least that was what she thought she must be doing. Because to her it felt more like she was being spun around by invisible hands.

There were sounds all around her. Strange noises that mixed and swirled about her mind. Filling it to the brim so that it pounded on every inch of her body to be free. It was a nightmare from which she could not wake.

Kritcha opened her eyes. What came through was an explosion of color and light. Green and brown and black flooded in, each edged in the horrible golden aura of a blinding sun that rocked her spinning mind. She twisted at the shock of it. Recoiled from the pain of its brilliance and fell to the ground. Her hands reached out, desperate to find any purchase. They found nothing.

She closed her eyes. Kritcha could see them as though they were standing before her. Her tiny brother and sister as they were pulled away. As the fire roared around her and the sound of their screams slowly died, she could feel the heat, remember the pain. She wanted to see them again. Not like this. She wanted to remember them happy. To see them playing again, to see their smiles and hear their laughs. Not faces contorted in terror or fading screams as they were taken away. She could see her friend, Calleh. A new face to add to her torment. A new scream to add to her own in the dark.

Friendly hands brought her up from the ground. They were rough hands, but they were free of sharp claws and pulled her up to set her walking again. They even helped for a little while to guide her, but soon they were forced away and the claws returned.

The smell of swamp filled her nostrils, polluting everything with its poisonous stench. A few times she vomited. Only there was nothing left, except bile and spit that came up at the smell.

She wanted to sleep. To be rid of the pain and the stench of the Laroo. Only they smelled so foul. Only they had such sharp, pointed fingers. They had caught her. They had poisoned her. She couldn't feel the dart, but she knew it was there. Yet she was still alive. Why would they keep her alive? And what hands were there that would keep the company of the Laroo to help her?

The only words she could think of came bursting out of her like blood from a fresh wound, "Green Boughs!"

～

STEN WATCHED as the webbed hand balled into a tight fist. It struck the woman in the cheek. Fresh blood oozed from her face. It was slow and thick, much darker than normal blood. She wouldn't last much longer. She stumbled forward, her own hands failing to catch her. Sten made an attempt, reaching out with his own bound hands to catch her. Then it was his turn to meet with the webbed fist.

"Warm blood, Warm blood, no touch old blood. *Gitcha, Gitcha, Gitcha.*"

The rest of the Hoppers took up the chorus.

Gitcha, Gitcha, Gitcha-a-Larooooooo!

Sten shook his head, trying to clear it after the blow. He had never been caught like this before. He had never been in so close a proximity to the Hoppers for so long. At least, while they were still alive.

Three of the soldiers had survived. Their hands and feet had been bound, and they shuffled along somewhere ahead of him. They didn't worry him though. It was the woman that concerned him. She was the only one of them who had caught a dart in the ambush. When she opened her eyes, the whites had gone the color of mud. She mumbled and screamed. Sometimes shouting. Which brought swift retribution from the Hoppers. Her face had become a bloody pulp from their blows.

It was a small face, almost pretty, but hard. Worn, but resilient. She couldn't have seen more than a score of seasons' turnings and yet her eyes, dark with the murk of the poison, spoke of age. She certainly couldn't have seen more than his thirty turns, and yet she looked as though she had seen more seasons than even the oldest could count. They looked out from a face tanned with the summer's sun. It was the face of someone who spent their time in the woods, amongst the birds and the beasts. A wild face. A strong face.

Her hair was brown, dark and deep as the bark of an ancient oak. He couldn't be sure, but he could swear that when the sun caught it just right, it shimmered green as though flecks of emerald had been sprinkled throughout. The unusual strands flowed like a river green and pure through the mud and blood, in long strands that reached past her thin shoulders.

The party stopped again. Another stream. It was like this at every one they crossed. The Hoppers would stop and play. Like horribly malformed children, they would wallow in the mire and coat themselves with mud. Only content when each was completely covered.

It was then that Sten tried, while they were distracted, to get some water to the woman. But she wouldn't drink. She would spit the water back out and shake her head, and when Sten tried to remove the dart his effort was met with hisses and a horrible chorus of *Gitcha, Gitcha, Gitcha-a-laroo!*

They moved at a crawl; many streams and rivers made for an almost glacial pace. The Hoppers really did love the mud. Sten began to wonder if they would ever get to where they were going.

"Green Boughs!" The woman shouted again. Her long muscular body contorted with the effort of the cry.

Sten jumped, her shout was so sudden and loud. It must have made the Hopper nearest her jump too because it opened its hand to strike her. But then it did a curious thing. The body moved forward as though still swinging at her, but the arm had stopped moving and was even going backwards. Then Sten saw it. The flash of steel retracted and the arm fell to the ground with a useless thump. The Hopper was as surprised as Sten at the sudden loss of its limb. It had no time to correct itself and carried the hollow blow through. It toppled forward catching the woman as it did. Digging its claws into her and pulling her to the ground.

Sten rushed forward, sliding through the fallen leaves to wrest her from its clutches as they grappled on the ground. He was stopped short, the press of razor steel at his throat and a voice low and cold in his ear.

"Stand away, southern soldier of the White Lily. Do

not touch the prize of the Lord of Green Boughs. We'll deal with the Hopper."

Sten forced himself up as best he could with bound hands and shuffled back from the tussle on the ground. The Hoppers hissed and called out as more men appeared. They pulled the woman away from the Hopper. One pulled back his hood.

"Get her help!" the figure shouted pointing at the woman. "And bring me the others."

Sten was pushed forward by a knife in his back. The other soldiers were brought up and forced to face the man.

"Where is Yit-Durdar?" he asked looking around at the Hoppers.

"Where is he? I was told he led the party north."

The Hoppers eyed each other nervously.

"Here, warm blood! Here!" the Hoppers parted as the largest Hopper Sten had ever seen came forward, flanked on either side by four others nearly as large. They each wore cloaks. Whereas the smaller Hoppers went bare. A rough patchwork of hide. Human hide. Taken from the bodies they ate. A couple wore helmets fashioned from multiple skulls bound together with sinew.

The one, the biggest one, loped forward. It's one good eye fixed on the man. The other was bound with some sort of bandage.

"What were you thinking?" the man asked, pointing to the woman.

"Bring her back alive. Do you not remember that, Durdar?" he walked over to her and rolled her over. The dart had broken off.

"You poisoned her, and then what? Thought she would be good practice as a punching bag?" He pulled what remained of the dart from her back, which was met with hisses and another chorus.

"Warm blood alive," Yit-Durdar said.

The man looked up at him.

"You're right. She is." The man turned toward the others and opened his mouth to speak, but Durdar beat him to it.

"Warm blood quick, Durdar need slow legs. Warm blood, old blood, not run now, no squirrelly whirly through the trees," Durdar glared at her with one good eye. "Squirrelly luck to have eyes, poke'em out, she poke mine." The Hopper mimed the action with two long claws and smiled.

"You won't be poking any eyes, Durdar. We need her intact, that was what we agreed to, wasn't it?"

The question hung for a moment, and the big Hopper stopped smiling.

"Pop eyes later, pop all the eyes then none can watch Durdar."

Sten wondered for a second what the brute meant and resolved to himself that he wouldn't be sleeping tonight or any night for that matter until he was rid of the big Hopper.

"I'm sure the Lord of Green Boughs will be very

pleased with your attempt at competence. Why didn't you try stabbing her a few times? That would have slowed her down too."

He leaned down over her.

"But it looks like you did try that," he said, examining a wound in her side.

"Who are they?" the man asked rising from the woman. He moved closer to Sten.

"Have I seen you before?"

Sten could barely remember the face, but with it so close to his own he started to recall.

"Strand? Leighman Strand?"

The man smiled. A cold, knowing smile.

"Stenwith Harrison. How have you found the north?"

Sten raised his hands showing the rope that bound them.

"The great huntsman, eh?" Strand motioned to Sten. "Do you know who you've captured?"

The great Hopper came closer. He stood almost as tall as Strand. Durdar looked over Sten with an appraising eye.

"Warm blood, no name to call." Yit-Durdar hopped back to where the cronies sat on their haunches.

"This is Stenwith Harrison." Strand gestured again to Sten. "The great Laroo hunter of the south. Sent by the queen herself, no doubt."

"What are you doing so far north, Leighman?" asked Sten.

"I could ask you the same thing, Stenwith. What right does the Queen of White Lilies believe she has to send hunters so far north? To send armies so far north? This is beyond her reach on a matter beyond her grasp. This is the land of the Lord of Green Boughs."

"How many Hoppers have you killed, Leighman?" asked Sten.

"Don't try it, Stenwith. It's already been done. They know what I was. They know what I did, why I came north. But I have earned their respect, at least as much as they're willing to give, but you, you have none of that. And respect from them is a small matter anyway; they hate us regardless. Isn't that right, Durdar?" Strand looked at Durdar. The giant Hopper just glared back at Sten, the cold wheels of its frog mind turning.

"So the real question becomes how many have you killed?" asked Strand, smiling at Sten as he did.

The big Hopper came closer again.

"Warm blood kill cousins? How many cold cousins warm blood kill?"

Sten hesitated, thinking for a moment about his predicament.

"What does it matter? They hate us anyway. I can see it in its eye, how succulent my flesh will be, how nice a cloak my skin will make."

"To them it does, because they won't let you go so easy as just killing you outright. They'll make sure you pay for each one you've killed."

"How many cold cousin huntman kill?"

Sten could see the anger growing in the Hopper. Maybe he thought it was best just to get the whole thing over with. Maybe honesty was the best policy.

"Four hundred," he said looking directly into the eye of the Hopper called Durdar. It was a trap, he thought. But Strand hadn't counted on his honesty. If he had lied or didn't answer at all they would still kill him, but the fewer he had killed would make him seem weaker in their frog eyes. They would hate him less. Now their hate would boil and fester like the fetid northern swamps they adored so much. Now it would be almost impossible for Strand to keep the Hopper from him.

"Kill warm blood!" Durdar cried, lunging at Sten. The Hopper's attack met with razor steel, rather than Sten's flesh.

"Not yet, Durdar. Green Boughs has an interest in this one too. He wants all the southerners he can get his hands on."

Sten did not take his eyes off the Hoppers. The trap was set. Now to wait and see which would spring it first. Sten began to feel the phantom pain in his missing fingers. It happened every time he set a trap about which he was uncertain. He remembered the one he had underestimated. The trap that had caught him and nearly cost him his life.

CHAPTER FIVE

The pace quickened with Strand leading the party. Whether it was fear or purpose that drove him, Sten couldn't say. For two days they went on. Heading north, deeper into the forests that covered the land.

Their journey was taking them toward the range of mountains known as the Wolf's Teeth, or in the words of the north Vulfeermus-Nigh. In ancient times the range had been the northern boundary of the Kingdom of Errandrim, when the Errandi had ruled, but that line was broken and the kingdom crumbling under the aegis of the White Lily. A queen who cared more for the dead than living. Who enjoyed chasing the shadows of the past more than caring for a kingdom or its people.

And yet Sten had served her, continued to serve her. He would do so, always. Because of what she had done for him. A favor he could never forget and a life he would live again, in peace. But first he had work to do, first he had to learn of the reason for the Hoppers' southward advance. He had to find the force driving them. Was it the loss of their southern cousins, which he had helped to hunt to near-extinction? Was it some northern lord with hungry ambition and a thirst for new land in a kingdom ripe for carving up? What was the intent of this Lord of Green Boughs and what did he want with the woman?

So many questions unanswered and so many more that he had found. His focus shifted back to the Hoppers that surrounded him. The cold Hopper eyes fixed on Sten, a mighty prize for a mighty fat frog.

The Hoppers tried to stop at each stream but were met with pointed words and sharpened steel at each attempt.

There was little conversation as they traveled. Only the cold glances of the one good Hopper eye at Sten, and the stares of Strand at Durdar making sure the Hopper didn't harm the huntsman.

They had to carry the woman now. Constantly tossing and turning, saying names Sten didn't know, punctuating muffled sentences with piercing screams. She was almost impossible to carry with bound hands. Wriggling more than a rabbit with its foot caught in a snare, they dropped her often.

Sten's focus, except for a few times when he could see the other soldiers, remained on her. Watching her

41

decay, helpless as her skin turned gray and then a dark brown. The wound in her side did not fester or rot. Some effect of the poison. Keeping everything else out so that only it could kill her.

In the shadow of Vulfeermus-Nigh, they stopped on the banks of a rocky stream. The Hoppers tried to play in their strange way but were only frustrated by its frigid temperature and the complete lack of mud.

"Warm blood! Warm blood! Why stop now? No mud, cold water," said Yit-Durdar. The great brute moped about like a child that couldn't get its way, splashing in the cold water, grumbling all the while.

"Not good for cold blood."

A chorus went up.

Gitcha, Gitcha, Gitcha, Gitcha-a-Laroooooo!

"We have to stop here, Durdar. The way to Ostenea-Bar is too dangerous to attempt at night. But if you would like to find a mire in which to wallow you're more than welcome," said Strand. He sat down on a rock and removed one of his boots.

Yit-Durdar looked at Strand with one bulbous frog eye and then to Sten. Sten met the look. He didn't blink. He didn't say a word. He just sat and waited for those cogs to turn, for the hatred that lingered just below that thin Hopper skin.

"Warm blood! Warm flesh! Die!" As Durdar spoke, four hands pulled at Sten.

They plucked him from the ground. Their long fingers wrapped around his arms, claws stinging him like so many angry bees. They pulled him up to face Durdar.

"Warm flesh. Warm cape," Durdar said, playing with his tunic of human flesh.

"Huntman make warm cape for Yit-Durdar. Huntman make helmet good for Yit-Durdar!" As it spoke the four cronies loped over and took up the chorus.

Gitcha, Gitcha, Gitcha-a-laroo!

Strand was up in an instant, his missing boot forgotten. But Strand's intervention was little help to Sten now. Hoppers seemed to come from everywhere. They poured out from behind ancient trees and clambered over the even-older rocks. Was this Durdars' trap? Had the Hopper mind turned the wheels to make this happen? Was this the reason why the brute had waited to come for Sten? Because the Hopper knew that Strand's men outnumbered its own? Sten wondered, but it did him little good to think of it now. His own trap had failed, as ill-conceived as it had been; now he was at their mercy. The Hopper was more devious than he had thought. The pain of his failure welled up in his missing fingers. The reminder of other failed traps.

"Warm blood. Warm blood. Strand not take warm blood from Yit-Durdar. All prize mine now. All prize for Green Boughs!"

Yit-Durdar advanced on Sten. The other Hoppers held Strand and his men at bay.

"Do you want to break the agreement with Green Boughs?" Strand yelled the question above the din of the Hoppers. He sounded strained, as though he was fighting back against them. Good luck, thought Sten, especially with only one boot.

"No break deal with Green Boughs. Only break huntman," said Durdar, smiling a toothy grin, filled with razor-sharp teeth.

Four more Hoppers that were as big as or nearly so big as Durdar loped into sight pushing the four smaller cronies out of the way.

Gitcha, Gitcha, Gitcha-a-laroooo!

Gitcha-Yit-Sonn-Gahrd, Gitcha-Yit-Sonn-Gahrd!

A strange call from the Hoppers. A new chorus. One that Sten had never heard before. Durdar advanced on him still smiling. The beast raised its pointed claws and clicked them together.

"Warm blood, warm flesh. Warm drink, warm cape."

The claws were at Sten's ears. Clicking their slow ominous rhythm. A long tongue slipped out from behind razor teeth. The smell of rot and swamp was overwhelming, being so close to the Hoppers, it was like a fog in the air. Sten could taste it. Their foul stench polluting everything. Sten's head began to droop, heavy with the stench of the Hoppers and exhaustion from the forced march north.

Sten tried to watch Durdar as it licked its teeth and lips.

"Bring warm squirrelly too! Bring woman! Durdar take the eyes of warm blood. She took mine I take hers," said Durdar still showing pointed teeth.

Then Durdar's tongue shot out, a slick, spittle-soaked harpoon. It wrapped around Sten's neck and, like a noose, tightened. Sten gasped, but there was nowhere for the air to go. The long, wet tongue stopped everything. The world continued to fade. Darkness slipped in, building from the edges, reaching for the center of his vision and thought with long arms, pulling him down. The last Sten saw of the world as his mind faded was the single eye of the great Hopper. Filled with what he could only describe as glee.

KRITCHA STOOD on the edge of a great, mist-covered swamp; her feet were wet, dark-brown water rose to her ankles. The whole thing tasted rotten, like stewed corpses, garnished with cedar boughs. Boughs. Boughs? Why could she remember boughs, not cedar, but boughs.

She could hear voices. Sounds like whispers in the trees, a wind in the cedars. Far off and distant, but familiar, so familiar. She heard a splash behind her. She spun about; there was nothing. No flash in the mist. No steps through the mire to signify a retreat. The pool there lay undisturbed.

She took a step, and her foot sank. Not far, just

enough for her to pull it back, fearing it would go further. She turned and tried another. It sank again just a little bit further this time. She heard another splash and looked up just in time to see a figure vanish into the mist. She took several steps toward it. Realizing only after the fifth step that she had sunk to the middle of her calf. The figure remained just out of her sight as she slogged forward. The splashes of its feet her only guide. She followed it, each step pulling her just a little farther, down into the mire.

Kritcha reached up to grab onto the branch of a cedar tree that arched above her. The branch snapped when she tried to pull herself up, and what little gain she had made was lost, plunging her even deeper into the cold mud.

The figure turned back to watch her struggle, it paused only for a moment. She couldn't see a face, only the shape of a body. Like smoke, it twisted in the mist. A dark black against the gray.

She pushed forward going ever lower into the swamp, which came to her chest now. Why wouldn't it stop? Why wouldn't it just let her see? She cried out, but silence was its only answer. The whispers of distant mouths her only comfort. She kept going, hoping to reach the figure. Hoping that it might stop to let her catch it. To let her see.

Only her head rose above the water. The figure stopped. It turned toward her again and slowly drew closer. She could see a face now. Her brother. Then her sister. Then her friend, and teacher, Calleh. The hollow eyes of the figure looked down at her. Each face still coming and going. They each smiled at her. Sad smiles, empty smiles.

It opened its mouth. From it came the sound of howling wind. The screams of all the Earth together. A hand slipped from the shade's form. It reached out to her, pushing her down, with a slow and deliberate motion. She tried to scream, to cry out. The swamp silenced her even before she had thought of the words to say. It flooded in, and the figure fell away.

She jumped. She was lying on the floor of a large chamber. There were men and Laroo all about her. Raised voices echoed around the chamber.

"Warm blood! Warm blood!" some Laroo shouted.

"What did you think would happen, Durdar?" said a man's voice, "That you would just be able to kill them?"

"Not let cold cousin killer live. Southern men bad! Southern men die," said the Laroo.

"I suppose that means us too? Remember what we —" he wasn't able to finish.

A resounding chorus went up.

Gitcha, Gitcha, Gitcha-a-Larooooo!

"Southern man Strand need remember where he is. North not so kind. North not so gentle. Warm blood weak as south," said the Laroo.

Again a chorus filled the space.

"We take man water hold. We make great hold of

Laroo. No southern queen stand then. No men stand anymore!"

Another chorus filled the room.

Kritcha sat up.

"And what will happen when they send an army?" asked the man's voice.

Her head was still spinning, but at least now she could see. The light didn't burn so badly as it had before. Men and Laroo occupied the chamber. Packed in tight they filled the space, which was, she noted, rather large. Old too. Older even than her own home maybe.

Moss hung down the walls. Pouring like water through holes in the vaulted ceiling. Torches placed in sconces lining the walls gave the chamber a dim yellow glow. There must have been fifty men and almost the same number of Laroo in the chamber. The place stank of swamp, but that was just the Laroo. She wondered how the men could stand to be so close to them for so long. She hadn't been awake five minutes, and she already wanted to hurl.

Kritcha placed her feet flat on the floor. The taste was strange. Not at all like cut stone. It tasted old like the dirt in the forest. It did not have the taste of rot and death like the fresh-cut stone of the cities. It was something else. Something she couldn't quite describe. Almost like the stone and the place itself had been twisted by some ancient malice. She shuddered at the thought. An action that must have been far more visible than she thought because a voice behind her whispered so close in her ear that it made her jump.

"I feel it too."

She had been so focused on the strangeness of the place that she had, for a moment, lost her sense of the beings about her. Except the living swamp called the Laroo.

"Feel what?" Kritcha asked. She turned to face the source. It was one of the southern soldiers.

"The strangeness of this place," he made a swirling motion with his head, "Something is wrong here...very wrong here."

"Who are you?" Kritcha asked, looking at the three of them all bound and sitting on the floor. There was another, but he was unconscious lying just a few feet from her.

"I'm Farrow. This," he gestured to the soldier on his right, "is Bremin." The black-haired soldier nodded. His long hair was matted and filled with all manner of sticks and leaves. His leather armor was black and steel-studded. Bearing no adornment or insignia. Southerner.

Farrow nodded to the soldier on his left, "This is Drummind." The soldier with short brown hair and the same black leather armor nodded at Kritcha.

"Do you know who that is?" she asked, nodding in the direction of the unconscious soldier.

"That," Farrow started, inching closer, "is Stenwith Harrison. The great Hopper hunter of the south. He was attached to our company just as we were marching north. They say there aren't enough Hoppers away south to hunt anymore. So the Queen of White Lilies is sending the hunters north." He paused. He was right in Kritcha's ear now.

"Which seems like it might not help much up here though."

And as if to punctuate his point another chorus rose from the Laroo.

"Warm blood learn of the strength of cold blood!" said the big Laroo.

"That one is Yit-Durdar," said Farrow motioning with bound hands to the big Laroo. "Their leader of sorts, I guess."

"I know that one," said Kritcha. "That's the one that killed my friend." She stopped. Eyes fixed on the great beast. Her mind on that night. The fire and her friend. The Laroo calling her name as she ran into the night.

"How do you know?" Farrow asked. Not taking his eyes from the big Laroo.

"It was my knife that took his eye," she said. Her eyes still fixed in space thinking back on that night.

Farrow gave her a doubtful look.

"You survived their attack? You're the one that killed two of them and wounded a third?"

Kritcha nodded slowly, her mind still back in that night; she could still feel the fear as she had run through the trees. That panic that had stricken her numb to all else but her will to survive. And now, now she was surrounded by the brutes. A raised voice, a man's voice brought her back to the chamber, brought her back to the room filled with her enemies and very few friends.

"You know she'll just send more! She won't stop until you're all gone. Look what she has managed to do in the south. We need to wait, Durdar. If you attack from the waters' hold they'll know something has changed. They won't stop then," said the man. Whom Kritcha noticed was only wearing one boot.

"Who is that man?" Krichta nodded at the man with one boot. "Why is he working with them?"

"That's Leighman Strand," said Farrow. "They seem to have some sort of deal. Beyond that I don't know why they're together here."

Kritcha nodded. She looked around the room; where were they? She had seen most of the old buildings in the forest south of the Wolf's Teeth, but this one was different; this one looked much older than any of the others she had seen. The stone, where not covered with moss or lichen, was almost black, granite or marble that must come from deep within the mountains.

She had heard rumors of men working with Laroo before. That on occasion they had formed alliances and fought together, but she had never seen it. She had hoped she never would. Why would men ally themselves with such foul creatures? What purpose could such an arrangement serve?

"Warm blood learn of the strength of cold blood! Warm blood learn tonight!" said Yit-Durdar, followed by a chorus.

Strand shook his head, pacing as best he could in the throng.

"And when the White Lily sends more soldiers? What will you do then, Durdar? In battle you cannot win. We need more men, more soldiers; steel and spears are the only thing that their armies will answer to. We need more of them before we make a move against the southerners. If we can gather everyone, if we can get the rest of the broken line to follow us... then we should strike."

"Warm blood take long. Destroy armies now that some warm blood magic gone from man water hold."

"Who are you?" Farrow asked, nudging Kritcha with his elbow.

"I'm nobody," Kritcha shrugged. "You can call me Kritcha."

"Kritcha? And you say you're the one that took Durdar's eye?"

Kritcha nodded.

"So you're the one they be must be after."

"After?" Kritcha asked, surprised.

"You were the only survivor. You were the one we were looking for too."

Kritcha turned away from Farrow and looked up. Every eye in the room was focused on her. The men's eyes were bad enough, but the black, bulbous frog eyes of the Laroo made her skin crawl. She wanted to run, to be free from the horrid stare and terrible stench. But where would she go? Where could she go? She was surrounded.

"Feeling better?" asked Strand.

"What does he mean? Looking for me? What do you want with me?" she asked, looking from Strand to the one good eye of Durdar.

"We need what only you can bring to us," said Strand, "We need—" his sentence was cut short by the sound of a wooden door banging hard on ancient stones.

"Your mother," said another voice. All eyes turned toward it. Kritcha felt a slight twinge of relief as the focus shifted elsewhere. She tried to see the source, but her view was obstructed by a forest of boots and legs.

"We need your mother, Kritcha," the voice said, though Kritcha still couldn't see the source. All around the room, men and Laroo alike bowed their heads. Who was this that even the Laroo bowed their heads to?

A man walked toward her. Slowly, almost regally. He wore long black robes. Unadorned except the green pine boughs that crossed his chest. He was tall and pale with black hair flecked with gray, like stars in a clear night sky.

"The Lord of Green Boughs?" Kritcha asked. The man nodded.

"My mother is dead. I watched her and my father

and my little brother and sister as they were dragged away," she nodded at the Laroo. "By them. Your *friends*."

"But was she really your mother?" the Lord of Green Boughs spoke softly. His voice was quiet and low; no one else made a sound so they could hear the man speak.

"Yes, she was. She raised me. Fed me. Protected me as best she could."

"All very nice things. But that does not make her your mother. I speak of the woman that conceived you, not she who raised you." The Lord of Green Boughs reached down and clutched at a lump that protruded from just above his stomach. He looked at Krticha as she watched him grab at the lump.

"Why would she come for me? If she is really my mother, why have I never seen her?"

"She doesn't like to show herself to her offspring. She doesn't like them to know what they are. She believes it keeps them safe, but we have ways of finding them. She was not so clever as she thinks."

"And what am I? Why would I need to be hidden?"

He walked closer to her and looked down at her with a wan smile.

"What am I?" she felt like she was being strangled, her throat closing in on itself. The room was spinning about her. Panic filled her voice as she shouted at the man.

"What am I!"

He smiled down at her, "You're what I need to take

back what is rightfully ours, and that is all that you need to know."

He turned and motioned to some of the men, "Put her with the others and take the four soldiers as well. We may still need them." He let go of the lump in his robes, but did not look away from Kritcha as she was hauled to her feet. She couldn't shake the feeling now. The brooding malice of the place that seemed to grow as she was dragged out past the Lord of Green Boughs.

"It doesn't matter if Durdar attacks now. We must have her mother... then nothing will matter."

"And what about the ambush, Lord?" asked Strand

"You are the hunter; you should have been more careful. You're lucky you were close to Ostenea-Bar, otherwise I might not have been able to help you at all."

The Lord of Green Boughs broke his gaze from Kritcha and looked over to where Sten was being hauled up.

"You southern hunters are proving less valuable and much less capable than I initially thought you would be."

Strand's face flushed, and he turned, storming from the room as best he could with only one boot.

Kritcha let herself be hauled out by the men. Watching as Green Boughs played with his lump again. The wooden door slammed shut behind them.

Who was her mother? What did they want with a

woman she didn't know? Why would she come for her now?

After the poison she felt as though she had been asleep for years. But now her mind was clear; the swamp was gone. Yet she had never been more confused.

CHAPTER SIX

K ritcha slumped down. Her back scraping against the moist, lichen-covered stone of the cell wall. She landed with a soft thump on the damp floor. She could hear but not see the others moving about in the dark. What little light there was didn't illuminate their faces or the cell, only a thin line below the door. Kritcha heard running water as though an underground river or stream ran nearby.

Voices in the hall caught her attention. Footsteps. Heavy steps, clad in iron-shod boots. They paused at her cell. Only for a moment.

"Which one's in here?" asked one of the voices. Low and gravelly. Like an old man's voice. Tinged with experience.

"Southern soldiers and one of the offspring," said a second voice. Higher, whiny. Almost prepubescent, probably didn't even need to shave.

"Why are we keeping the soldiers?" asked the old man. Boots hitting ancient stone. The pair had started walking again.

"The soldiers are as insurance or something like that. Something about a southern queen I think. The one is a hunter from down south like Strand. The Lord thinks he might help in finding more offspring from that bitch," said the little-boy voice.

"You kiss your mother with that mouth of yours, Little Hem?" There was a sound of a hand slapped on leather.

"No, you big old brute." There was another sound of slapped leather. "She's dead," said Hem.

"And you still kiss 'er. How sick are you, you skinny little runt."

"Not as sick as you, Ley, I've seen what you've been doing to the other offspring."

"Gotta get my kicks somehow, boy. And they're all so weak, just prime for the pluckin'."

"And the fuckin'?"

"You keep your damn mouth shut, boy." There was another blow, this time harder, and it sounded to Kritcha like one of them ran into a wall. "I done nothin' of the sort."

"Sure." Another blow echoed from the hall.

"How many more did the whore have?" asked Ley. "We already have eight of them. I'm sick of watching them or..." there was a sound of a fist knocking on wood. "...what's left of them."

"You'd think that if she cared about them, she'd have come for them by now," said Hem.

"Hah," Ley scoffed. "Those things don't care about their children. You know what she is, don't you?"

The voices were getting quieter. Receding into the distance.

"Ya know why he wants her, don't you?" said Ley. Kritcha scooted to the door putting her head to the gap at the bottom, listening at the crack. They must have turned a corner because she couldn't hear them anymore.

Eight of them? There were more like her? What were they? What was she? Her head was spinning again, but not from poison this time. As the questions swirled around, she raised her head.

"It's not right." The voice in her ear made her jump. It was Farrow, or at least it sounded like him.

"Sorry," he said scooting closer. "I've felt it since we got here. Something strange, something old." He looked around as he spoke, whispering. As though he didn't want whatever they felt to hear him. Kritcha could barely see his face in the dark; it looked like a pale ghost hanging in the air, no body to support it.

Kritcha turned to him. "Did you feel it more when you were by Green Boughs?"

Farrow nodded. "It's the lump," he shuddered. "The way he looked at you when you caught him playing with it."

"What do you think it is?" Kritcha asked, looking in

what she thought to be the direction of the unconscious hunter.

"I have no idea," said Farrow. "Maybe it's some deformity. Some growth. My grandmother," Farrow swallowed. "She used to tell us stories about creatures that could take limbs, arms, legs, whatever they wanted really...and..."

"What?" Kritcha asked.

"Could make all kinds of awful things..." said one of the other soldiers.

"Men with ten heads and twenty arms and thirty legs..." said the other.

"But that wasn't the worst..." Farrow said.

"What was it? What else did they do?" asked Kritcha, her curiosity bubbling out, like water from a spring. "If he could do that, then why hasn't he? Why would he need a woman who's supposed to be my mother? What use could she be, whoever she is to him?"

"I don't know," said Farrow. "Maybe he's not what we think he is, but if he is...there is a madness that comes with the weld."

"Weld? What is the weld?" asked Kritcha.

"It's what the Sangunists, blood workers, they used it when they twisted themselves. The weld blood. Weldlings."

"Weldlings?" Kritcha asked.

"They could make things..." Farrow paused and swallowed hard in the dark. "Creatures, nasty things."

"What's nastier than a Laroo?" she asked.

Farrow shook his head as though he was trying to forget something.

"Maybe it's something else. Those were just stories to scare little children, you know like the Hoppers, sneaking in at night to steal bad little children or the Grom-Lic, coming to take our bones and grind them to powder with his stone teeth, to make us behave."

"They didn't tell us stories to scare us. They told us to warn us, to keep our doors shut and to put our fires out at night. Because they would find us if we didn't, but that was the way. The Laroo always just waiting to take us away at night, and I don't know what a Grom-Lic is. I guess I missed that story. All I know is that we have to get out of here. This Lord of Green Boughs won't be able to hold back the Laroo for very long, and when they come we had better not be here."

"Agreed," said Farrow. "But how do you suppose we'll do that?"

Kritcha reached her hand under the door. She gave the ancient lumber a few hard tugs. It was old, but surprisingly solid. She turned back to the dark interior of the cell. She scooted closer to the far wall. Never standing, just skittering across the floor, like a spider in the dark. She had to maneuver over the unconscious hunter as she did; it took her a second to orient the direction of his body. Once she did, she was able to get over him and make it to what she guessed was the rear wall of the cell. The sound of water grew louder the closer to the wall she got. She pressed her ear to the cool, damp stone and listened. It sounded as though the water was close on the other side. She moved to a crouch, pressing her hands against the wall.

The floor tasted different here. It didn't have the quality of the cut stone in the rest of the cell. This stone tasted fresh. Though much older, it wasn't cut like the rest. It was still alive, still a part of the living earth. It was smooth too. Very smooth. With small holes cut in it. The kind formed by running water. Her heart leapt at the thought. If the water could find its way in. Then maybe they could find their way out.

She ran her hands over the wall. Built partially of cut stone and also of the living rock, she could find no hole where the water might enter. Kritcha kept up the task for several minutes before there was movement behind her.

"Farrow?" she asked, having momentarily forgotten the others. "Farrow, come here and help me. I think I might have found our way out." There was no answer. She turned from the wall.

"What's going on?" Her eyes scanned the dark.

"He's waking up," said Farrow.

She moved in the direction of his voice but collided with one of the other soldiers as she did. With a curse she was over the soldier and near to what she guessed to be the hunter's side.

"What—" the hunter swallowed. "Happened?" he asked, his voice just a whisper.

"How did—" he swallowed again.

"Green Boughs saved you from the big Hopper. Saved us all," said Farrow. "I don't think the big brute is finished. He said something about an eye for the one you took, Kritcha, and another just for fun. We need to get out of here before he takes the opportunity."

"Where...are...we?" the huntsman asked. Each time he spoke it was slow and laborious.

"Enjoying the hospitality of the Lord of Green Boughs," said Kritcha.

"Who—" started the huntsman, but Kritcha cut him off.

"The one you strung up in a tree. My name is Kritcha."

"Why...still alive" asked the huntsman.

"I don't know what he wants with you; maybe it's the same reason he has Strand working for him. Maybe he thinks you'll help him look for the others like me, I don't know, but I personally don't care to find out. Do you?" She let the question hang in the dark.

Her mind drifted back to the floor with its water-washed holes. She wanted to know the answer to those questions. She wanted to know why they had gone through so much trouble to find and keep her alive. She wanted to know who this woman was who was supposed to be her mother, but she wanted to be free to do it on *her* terms. She didn't like being trapped like this. She needed to get out.

The huntsman grabbed her in the dark. His hands were cold and clammy. She shook the touch off.

"Why...do..."

"Something about my *real* mother something about what they can make her do to release me and the others like me."

"Others...like...you?" the huntsman asked.

Kritcha hesitated. She had always been told it was just a trait of some northerners, that she was just a holdover from a by-gone age when the world and its people were one. That she could taste and sense things others couldn't because she was more in tune with the world, because she had lived alone in it for so long she had become more a part of it. That's what Calleh had told her, and she had believed him. It had made sense to her then, but maybe that was because she had wanted it to make sense, needed it to make sense. Because she had wanted an explanation, but not one that made her different, just one that gave her comfort.

But now she knew different. Calleh had, even though it was to make her feel like she belonged, lied to her. She was different, but what was she? Why did they want her mother, whoever she was?

"Real...mother...?"

The huntsman's question brought her meandering mind back from its wanderings in the mire of the past. She looked in the direction of his voice.

"I don't know why they want her. To be honest I don't even know who or what she or I am, or why we are so important to this strange, lumpy, forest lord. I need to get out of here, then I'll worry about all of that. I want answers, but now, with those very angry Laroo waiting just outside, is not the time. I'll get them later, when I'm safely away from this place."

"We...all...do..." said the huntsman. "Hoppers...come...for...us." He swallowed hard at the effort of speaking.

"What were you saying, Kritcha?" asked Farrow. "About the wall?"

"I think the river on the other side sometimes overflows. It might have eaten through the mortar of the cut stone. If we can find a hole we might be able to pry the cut blocks loose and get through."

"Then?" asked the huntsman.

"If we can find a hole then we'll worry about what comes next. If we don't, next won't matter," she said, moving back to the wall rubbing her hands over the damp surface.

In a few minutes they were all rubbing their hands over the rear wall of the cell, like five blind squirrels, searching for a lost acorn. After long desperate minutes, there was a grunt.

"Here," the whispered voice of the huntsman. "Loose," he said.

There was a scramble as everyone crowded around him, each prying and scraping, trying to get the stones loose. Kritcha stopped for a second. She thought she could hear something else. Like a cry, then a whimper in the distance. She moved to the door, crouching near the gap at the bottom, but it was gone. The sound of the river grew much louder. She turned towards the group working at the wall.

"Did you get one out?" she asked, scooting back over to them.

"Yeah," said Farrow. "But the farther up we go the more difficult it gets; the river must not get that deep when it does overflow. We may need another option or get very thin."

"If we're in here long enough I would imagine the second option might be doable," she said, going back to the door trying to hear the cries in the distance. Now she could hear something else over the flow of the river.

Kritcha listened at the door. She could hear footsteps in the distance. They weren't the thud of the soldiers' heavy iron-shod boots. She turned to the others, hissing at them to be quiet. All four stopped; only the huntsman moved closer.

"What..." He paused, swallowing hard. "Is it?" he whispered in her ear.

She shook her head, moving it closer to the gap at the bottom of the door. The huntsman did the same.

It sounded almost like something was scraping against the ancient stones. Like nails...or long claws.

There was a sudden burst of speed from outside the door as the slow laborious steps broke into gallop.

Kritcha pulled the huntsman back as something

big collided with the door. Stenwith looked at her, his face a pale shadow in the light from the gap. He looked old. Older than she had imagined from his voice. There were deep scars, that even in the dim light were clear on his face. She ignored the implication of the look and moved back, getting as far from the door as the cell would allow. Another blow shook the door. Which for its age held very well against the Laroo's heavy blows.

"What is it?" asked Farrow, his voice a shaking whisper in her ear. Some soldier, she thought.

"Laroo," she whispered back.

Again, the door shook with a blow from outside. Kritcha moved to the side of the cell with the most space between her and the door. Another blow. It was almost through. The door had little resistance left to give. Light shone through where splinters had broken loose. She poised herself. Coiled with the palms of her hands flat against the moist wall. Crouched, ready to burst through at whatever it was that came through the door. She couldn't see the others. It didn't matter. If she could make it through, that was all that mattered.

The door exploded inward. In an instant, she was on top of whatever Laroo had come through the door. It was slippery, like trying to get a firm grip on a greased melon. Somehow she did. For a few moments she held on and twisted with the thing. After a few seconds, it gained its feet and launched back into the wall, smashing Kritcha into the ancient stones. The blow caused her to release her grip, and the brute rounded on her. Pinning her to the wall with long claws. She watched, helpless, as the big one lumbered in.

It looked at her, then at Sten.

"Warm blood. Old blood. Both prize now," said Yit-Durdar. "Eye for an eye not make world blind, only warm blood go blind. First take eyes then take life. "It hopped over to her.

"Easy catch squirrel, no trees for it to run in," the big brute Durdar said, clicking its claws and presenting a grin filled with razor-sharp teeth.

"Mother no come for little squirrel buried down deep. No come for little squirrel now." Its claws extended out toward her face.

"Not take just one. Make little squirrel blind. Then little squirrel respect Yit-Durdar."

She hadn't fought once the thing had her. She hadn't struggled. She had waited and as the claws drew closer to plucking her eyes from their sockets she pulled to the side. The smaller Laroo, not expecting the sudden movement, lost its grip and she lashed out. Kicking and punching whatever her hands and feet could find, a dervish of primal fury.

Seizing upon the confusion, the huntsman struck the Laroo that held him, breaking the hold of his own captor, sending the startled Laroo flying. He launched himself at the biggest one. The pair careened off the walls, colliding with the other soldiers and Laroo alike, as they grappled in the tiny cell.

She struggled against two of the Laroo, still a blur of hands and feet. She pummeled one so that it fell back into another Laroo. With a kick from one of the soldiers, the pair of frogs were propelled into the hallway. She turned just in time to see the huntsman and the big Laroo plow into the back wall of the cell.

The ancient stones at the back of the cell fell away with force of the collision. Stenwith and the great Laroo disappeared into the gloom beyond. Farrow and the others still struggled with Durdar's cronies. Kritcha rushed toward the gaping hole in the cell wall. The sound of water thundered now, the river running past in the dark, what she hoped was only a few feet below. Stenwith and Durdar had vanished into the roiling tumult of the water, their bodies swept away to be battered upon the jagged rocks.

Kritcha looked back considering the alternative to the water below. The open door and warm light of the torch beyond. It called to her, beckoning her to find safety in its warm light. She hesitated, considering each. As she did, the hand of the Laroo she had knocked down reached up, raking its long claws across her side. She sprang forward. Leaping headlong into the water below.

CHAPTER SEVEN

Sten struggled against both the creature and the current. Fighting for breath. Fighting for his life. He propelled himself what he hoped was up, toward the surface of the frigid river.

He gasped for air but swallowed nearly as much of the river as he did air. Long claws raked his face and neck, back and sides. The great brute had nearly wrapped itself around him in a great, macabre hug.

Fighting a Hopper in water was like trying to wrestle a greased bear into a dress. No matter what he grabbed, it slipped through his fingers and the thing was nothing but teeth and claws.

One thing that was different was that at least with the bear neither fighter was happy. But with the Hopper, Sten knew the thing was delighted to have him on its turf.

Sten's head plunged back under the icy water of the

underground river. He wondered, if only for the briefest of moments, where the river emerged if at all, from the ground. He had to get to land; he had to get where he at least stood a chance. He still might not have the advantage on land, but at least he could hold his own.

In the water he was as good as dead. The thing was smart and strong, much smarter than he had ever given Hoppers credit for being.

The brute made sure each time they came to a boulder or obstruction that it put Sten's body between it and the stone, using Sten's body as a buffer. Each time his body hit another rock his mind clouded a little more. He had to get out of the water or this thing, and the river with it, would kill him.

Sten noticed a pattern that whenever there was something coming the brute scrambled to reverse itself and pushed Sten to an arm's-length to lessen the blow it received.

He waited until the brute did it again and hoped that he could time it out just right. He knew he would only have one chance to get it right because once he tried it the big Hopper would expect it the next time.

He forced his way back up. More by the virtue of another collision than by his own effort, but he would take it. The current was slowing. Which was both good and bad. Good in that it meant he wouldn't have his head bashed by a rock but also bad in that Sten had hoped he could get a blow in on the brute.

He took in as much air as he could before they both went under again.

Sten managed to get himself into a ball, which helped him to sink faster in what seemed like an underground lake, but he also noticed something else.

The longer they were in the water the slower the big brute moved. Cold blood not so good in cold water.

Sten kicked his legs out catching the brute square in the middle of its big body. An action that to Sten's delight had the effect of both momentarily stunning the Hopper and propelling him toward the surface of the underground lake.

He kicked his legs as hard as he could, while using his arms to pull himself upward. He had to move quickly if he wanted to get away from the thing—the cold would only slow it a little. He could already feel its effects on his own body, but he pushed through, the fire of adrenaline burned through the cold. Fear gave him strength.

Sten broke the surface of the lake. He filled his lungs with air and kept paddling, as hard as he could toward what he thought was the glow of a lit torch around the next corner. With each stroke he expected the claws of the brute Durdar to reach up and grab him, but to his surprise no claws reached up for him, no Hopper hands, such as they were, wrapped around his ankles.

He kept swimming. Stroking toward the light he hoped would bring with it a human face. Rounding the corner, he saw the shape of a man standing next to the water. A soldier. But at least it was human.

Sten pulled himself up onto the ledge. The soldier came closer to him.

"Ey, what you doin' in the water. Don't you know that'll kill you; it's too cold to go swimming in."

Sten coughed up some of the rivers water and laughed, "You don't know the half— "

A fist slammed into his side, knocking him from the ledge. With a grunt and a splash, Sten unceremoniously reentered the frigid water of the river from which he had only briefly been free.

He tumbled against the force of the blow and tried to kick the Hopper. A few of his blows hit home, and the Hopper writhed, but they weren't enough to stop the thing, which came on like a rat after a fetid corpse, it was all teeth and claws, sharp and furious. A hungry lust burned in its one eye—Sten caught glimpses of its darkness through the river's crystal water.

The brute shoved him into another rock and what clarity he had gained from his brief respite was obliterated in an instant. His mind reeled from the blow, but he was not out of the fight yet. He had to remember the pattern; he could get the thing, he just had to time it right. The blow he knew wouldn't stop the thing, he had taken several and was still conscious, but it might give him enough time to make it ashore.

The river was getting rougher again. Narrower and faster with more rocks, most he managed to dodge.

The cold had slowed the creature down even more than it had slowed his own faculties. It was now or never. He had to get the brute.

The beast pushed him, its hands and feet in the middle of his chest. There had to be another rock coming. Sten rolled back so that his head was pointed almost directly downstream. He extended his arms in a wide sweep that met above his head in a fully extended clap.

The motion threw the Hopper off, which had not expected him to move, and instead assumed he would just take the beating as he had before. The thing tried to reposition itself, but Sten wrapped his arms around its mid-section and held with all the strength he still possessed.

Sten felt the impact as the Hopper shuddered to a brief halt before bouncing back into the current. He released his grip and, with both feet, kicked off from the thing. Its long claw tipped fingers reached out for him, but they only managed to scrape his ankles as he swam as hard as he could away from the thing.

He moved quickly, trying to put as much distance as he could between himself and the big Hopper. He pushed off rocks bounding down the river, and he swore that there was light ahead. Not the yellow glow of a torch, but the white radiance of the sun.

Sten's heart leapt at the thought, and he paddled harder. It gave him hope, scant though it was. It was the only hope he had. But hope, he knew, was fickle and like fate played games with the desperate mind. As he drew near, he noticed that the glow was coming from below the surface of the river. Before he could discern the nature of his next predicament he slipped over the edge of the water-fall and plummeted into the nothing below.

CHAPTER EIGHT

Plunging into the frigid water her world went dark, the warm glow of the torch beyond the door a distant memory. One obliterated by the sudden rush of icy water. She struggled to pull herself above the surface, but each time she came close she was pulled under again to be bashed against another rock. She fought for air; she only found more water.

After what felt like hours being battered in the river, the current slowed, and at last she was able to make her way to the surface. Though still pushed by the current, she was at least able to get a look at the caves around her. Most of which was shrouded in darkness with a few shafts of light that punctuated here and there where water had worn through the crust of the Earth.

She let the current drive her, wondering where, if at all, the river emerged from the Earth. Also if the huntsman and the Laroo were still grappling some-where ahead, or if the Laroo had already bested the huntsman and was waiting for the rest to follow the river down.

Kritcha rounded a corner, and she caught a glimpse of a yellow light ahead. She started stroking to pull herself closer to the light. Her arms were heavy, as though she was trying to paddle with two dead logs. Soon she wouldn't be able to move them at all or her legs for the matter. She had to get out of the water.

The light was getting brighter. She was almost there. As she drew near she could see the silhouette of a man. Was it the huntsman? The Laroo? Was it another soldier keeping watch in the dark? It was looking into the water. Looking right at her. She tried to duck under but realized that if she did she might not be able to pull herself back from the depths of the icy river.

So she drifted, directing herself as best she could with numb arms and legs. With all her strength she flung an arm out of the water. Her numb fingers groped frantically at the figure's boot. It shrieked and cried out at her.

"Hoppers don't like cold water, what are you doing in here?" he was still backing away from her. Taking the light with him as he went. Kritcha clawed at the stone, her numb hands slipping on the wet surface, hardly able to obey her commands. She twisted and wriggled, flopping about like a demented fish trying to kill itself, half in the water, half on the stone ledge.

"Get out of 'ere, bloody Hopper!"

The man was gaining some measure of composure. He moved closer to her. He must not be able to tell what she really was in the dark. He still thought she was one of the Laroo.

"What are you?" he peered down at her, taking several steps closer. He drew steel. She could almost reach him. Another step.

He raised the sword, making to strike her. "I'll send ya back to the Lord in pieces."

Kritcha swung her arm out and with her clumsy fingers she latched onto his boot. She pulled as hard as she could, bringing herself up onto the rocks and pulling the man down at the same time.

She was shaking violently. She had to keep moving. She had to get out of the dark. She thought for a moment about the other soldiers. There was little she could do for them now. They were, like her, on their own.

CHAPTER NINE

Kritcha rubbed her arms and legs watching as the pool of blood under the man's head grew deeper. He wouldn't be a problem and would even be rather generous in death. She liberated him of his steel. Just a short sword and knife, but even those were better than nothing if the rest of the Laroo had decided to brave the frigid water.

The torch was still burning too. Very generous indeed.

Stone steps cut from the living rock ascended into darkness. She looked around and seeing no other course moved up them into the dark.

She walked up the slick stone steps as quietly as she could. Careful not to slip on the wet stone as she did. The frigid memory of the icy water clung to her and, like a bad dream that wouldn't be shaken free, pervaded her entire being. From her soggy head to her bare toes she shook violently. So much that it was diffi-cult to hold the torch or lift her legs to take the next step forward.

She staggered back, her head spinning. Maybe it was some trace of the poison still clinging to her, or maybe it was exhaustion and the lack of food. Her stomach growled, low and angry. She was so hungry.

She reached out and with her thick, clumsy fingers, groping the slick stone of the passage wall. For a moment she held, but her grip didn't last long; she was too cold, too numb. Her hand slipped off the wall, and she swung the other over to catch herself, forgetting for a moment that it held the torch. She slammed it against the wall of the passage; hot ash exploded from the torch, covering her arm and hand. As quick as she could she moved to brush it off. Her head was still spinning, so instead of brushing the ash from her arm she fought to keep herself from falling back down the stairs, forced to let the hot embers burrow their way into her skin.

Her stomach growled again as her head cleared. She needed food, needed to get out of this place. She forced herself forward, fighting back the traces of dizzi-ness that waited on the fringes, like a mid-morning fog that refused to surrender to the rising sun. Reminding her that at any moment she could be thrown, by a fit of her own mind, down the slick stairs to her doom.

She walked upward, her pace painful and slow. Bright mushrooms clung to the walls of the passage.

Her mouth watered at them, at the thought of what they could make. A nice stew maybe. Piping hot and filled to the brim with potatoes and carrots, onions, and mushrooms slathered in thick gravy. Kritcha noticed she had stopped and was staring at the mushrooms, which in the glow of the torch looked almost pretty. Bright blues and greens and oranges. She shook her head, trying to rid herself of the thought of stew. She wasn't likely to find something like that here. A crust of moldy bread, a scrap of old jerky. Even a plump, juicy slug or slow-moving spider would do the trick right now. To her and her angry stomach's dismay, there weren't even any of those to be found.

She forced herself past the mushrooms. Pretty ones were usually the worst. At least to eat. Funny how they were like people. Not that she had eaten any pretty people. She had, however, eaten pretty mushrooms, and they, like people, had left a bad taste in her mouth and churned her stomach for a week. She shook her head again, breaking the chain that had dragged her thoughts so far from her current predicament.

Kritcha made progress. Slowly. Her stomach groaning out to be sated of its desires. For now, she had to ignore it. From time to time a wave of dizziness washed over her, and she was forced to stop and catch herself. Her side burned from where the long Laroo claws had scraped across her skin. Strange, she thought, that it wasn't worse, that her blood hadn't gone completely sour.

She climbed up for what seemed like ages. Each twist bringing more stairs that she needed to navigate. She went around one, then another and another; each one looked the same. The tantalizing thought of mushrooms were renewed with each step. As her mind drifted to far-off stews and fat grubs, she heard something, like a whine, distant and high.

Kritcha moved a little faster, as fast as her weak body would allow. The whine grew louder, and she realized that it was sobbing. A high-pitched continuous cry that echoed off the walls. She ran now, or at least to her mind what felt like running. The walls became a blur, a rainbow created by the passing mushrooms.

The wind roared in her ears blocking out the sound of the crying for a time. She stopped, listening. It was much louder now. She was very close. There was light coming from somewhere up ahead. She set the torch down gently. Other voices rose over the wailing sobs of whatever poor creature they emanated from.

"Get up!" a voice shouted. "Worthless!"

Kritcha inched closer, her back against the wall of an ancient cut-stone corridor. Hunger forgotten for the moment, her heart racing.

"The lord wants to talk to you, worthless lump!" there was shuffling. The scrape of boots on stone and still the wailing persisted.

"Come on you, get up!" the same voice shouted. "You'll have to help me. Grab its other arm."

"I ain't touching that thing. You know what happens if you touch one?" said a second voice. It sounded vaguely familiar.

"No, but I do know what will happen if you don't," said the first voice. It had to be the same two guards. What were their names again? She wracked her tired brain. Hem, little boy, that was the second voice, and Ley, the old man. The one that liked to touch.

"Oh yeah?" asked Hem. "What's that?"

"I'll cut off your lousy hands," said Ley.

"You wouldn't do that," said Hem.

"I will. Then we'll see if you can still find a way to play with yourself at night."

Kritcha could see a door now. Like the one to the cell she had been held in. Ancient but sturdy, flung wide open.

"Wait, you know abou—" but Ley cut him off.

"Thought I was asleep, didn't you? Pervert. You know if you beat it like that it'll fall off, right?"

"What?" said Hem, genuine surprise in his voice.

Kritcha pressed her back against the door, still listening to the two banter.

"Come on pick it up." There was a grunt.

"Will it really fall off?" Hem asked with a grunt.

"And whoever Ameler is won't be happy about an ugly boy that beat his own cock so much it fell off. Not that she would let you wriggle on top of her anyway," said Ley.

"It won't fall off, and she would love me anyway," said Hem.

"Keep telling yourself that and see if she stays when you can't give her any little kiddos to suck on her sagging teats."

"Sagging? There are none firmer, and she's not a cow. Don't call them teats."

"Heh, wait till she pops out a couple, then you'll see how firm they stay."

Kritcha peered around the corner. Their backs were toward her. That always made it easier. An unsuspecting man was always much easier to kill. It wasn't honorable or honest to stab a man in the back, but in matters of life and death, honor or honesty seldom crossed her mind. She found that those who were supposed to be more honorable were not, and those who were not expected to be were even worse. Her own honor was not something that often troubled her. Such things only hindered the hand and mind. Her hands needed to be free and her mind clear if she was to survive.

They were lifting a rather pathetic-looking person, who was more bone than flesh. Kritcha wondered for a moment if it was one of what the guards had called the offspring. She realized, as they began dragging the body towards the door of the cell, that she didn't have time to wonder.

She pulled the knife from her borrowed belt and stepped around the corner. She drew the short sword.

Pausing for a moment, she wondered if she had the strength to drive the blades to a killing blow. She chased the thought from her mind and raised up the sword and knife.

With her left hand she reached around and slit one guard's throat; it was Ley, the old man. She figured that experience should go first, as he might react with more clarity than the boy when confronted with danger. Ley and the knife fell to the floor. He clutched at his throat, blood pouring through his fingers as he tried to stem the flow. It was a pointless endeavor. He gargled on his own blood; soon he would drown in it.

Hem turned toward her, a look of shock on his face. She stuck the sword into his throat; he didn't even have time to scream. She pulled the blade free as he too fell to the ground. The other was still struggling. Holding his throat and gasping for air. He wouldn't last much longer, but old Ley had gone on much longer than she had expected. She wiped her blades on his clothes as she watched the life fade from his eyes.

Hem really was just a boy. Tall, but still young. He did need to shave though, a shadow of a beard that a hard scrubbing might have removed, clung to his slender face.

She looked down at the other figure. The limp form of the prisoner slumped on the floor where the guards had dropped it. It had ceased its crying but continued to whimper. She rolled it on to its back. Its eyes were hazy, and they didn't focus on her like eyes normally did when presented with a new subject. They just stared straight ahead as though they couldn't see her.

"Who are you?" Kritcha asked. It jumped, startled at a new voice.

It said nothing.

"Why do they want us?" Kritcha asked.

"Mother, they want a mother. My mother is dead, when I was young," it said, its eyes still not focused.

"Who is she? Why do they want her?" Kritcha asked.

"The Laroo, she can help them. The waters' hold. That's what he said." Its eyes were moving faster now, darting about the room, seeing nothing. "They would use it. To make an army. To get revenge. The Queen of White Lilies."

Kritcha heard footsteps in the distance. Iron-shod boots. More men.

"White Lilies! White Lilies! White Lilies!" it shouted. The steps broke into a run.

"Why?" she asked, panic rising in her voice.

"Old blood." It shook its head violently. Almost as though it was trying to convince itself more than her.

Kritcha stood. Taking up her steel she pressed herself flat against the wall of the cell nearest the door.

Three men burst into the room. Two clad in dark brown cloaks carrying long spears. The third wore black robes and had...

"The Lord of Green Boughs," Kritcha whispered,

but in so small a place it was enough. He turned to face her. She glanced at his lump and without hesitation lashed out at the nearest soldier. Catching him in the side before he could turn to face her. She left the knife and propelled herself through the open door. Careening off the wall opposite the door, she tore down the corridor. Running with all the strength her tired legs and starving body could muster.

CHAPTER TEN

Kritcha ran. Her heart pounding in her ears, but not so loud that she couldn't hear the Lord of Green Boughs yelling after her.

"Where are you going to go? Can you find your way out of here?"

He was right. How was she going to find her way out? The question burned in her mind, an ember that set light to the pyre of despair that had been growing. All she knew was that she had to keep going, so, she did what she knew best. She ran for her life. Just as she had when the Laroo had killed Calleh. She had escaped that trap, and she would escape this place, of that much she was certain.

Down the corridor she sprinted, the fire of fear driving her exhausted body forward beyond what she thought possible. The deep scratches where the Laroo had clawed at her throbbed, but she kept focused, kept forcing herself forward.

The corridor before her split in two directions, one to her right and one to her left. She paused for a moment considering which to take. The one on the right was darkened and the left lit. The sound of heavy boots behind her forced a decision. She went left not knowing where either would lead. At least she could see where she was going.

Doors flew past her, a blur of brown and black. There were dozens of them, and she wondered briefly what lay beyond each one. Maybe a way out. She slowed her pace and reached for one of them. She tried the latch. Locked. She tried another and another; they were all locked. She didn't have time to try each one—she had to keep moving. Sweat beaded on her brow, frustration filled her mind, edging out the fear of what followed her.

She kept going, not knowing where she would end up. Each time she paused to try and catch her breath she could hear the distant sound of boots on stone. She had to find her way out of this place, but it was a labyrinth, an endless maze of corridors. One lead to another and another, and they all looked nearly identical. Ancient stone lit with the light of torches in rusted sconces. Wooden doors built of ancient timber.

She stopped and listened. She couldn't hear the boots anymore, but there were voices. They weren't shouting though; they were talking low and calm. A normal conversation. She couldn't discern what they were saying, so she edged closer, moving towards the voices down the hall, careful not to make a sound.

Drawing the sword, she had liberated from the guard by the river she rounded a corner and peered into the next corridor.

There were three soldiers. Two had their backs to her the other was holding something, his eyes were focused on it. Kritcha pulled her head back around the corner while trying to listen to the conversation. Their voices still sounded muffled, and she caught only pieces of what the trio was saying to one another.

Something about the old blood. An ancient war. Moving south soon? She couldn't be sure. An edge. Edge of what? Just as she worked up the courage to look around the corner again, her angry stomach let out a growl and one of the soldiers glanced back toward her.

"Did you hear something?" he asked. The other two shook their heads.

"Don't worry. It's just this old place, full of all kind of strange sounds."

He turned back to the other two. Kritcha let out a sigh. She would have to find another way around. As she started back down the corridor she heard heavy boots on stone and the shouts of her pursuers.

Now she had no choice. It was forward or nothing.

At least she had the element of surprise on the three around the corner.

Sword in hand she took a depth breath, closed her eyes to steady her nerves. Her stomach let out another angry rumble.

It was now or never. She opened her eyes and peeked around the corner. They hadn't heard the shouts yet or they were ignoring them. She wasn't sure; maybe they were passing them off as just more noise from the old halls, it didn't matter.

She raised the sword and charged, headlong down the corridor. The one soldier facing her started to cry out, but she was already on top of them.

Sharpened steel penetrated one's spine. Blood rushed from his throat in a gush of red, like the bursting of a dam upon the floor, great rivulets pouring forth, soaking his body. If only she hadn't dropped the knife she might have taken two at once. Such as it was she used her left fist to break the nose of the soldier facing her as he tried to cry out. The soldier to her left turned, a look of shock and horror on his face.

The momentum of her attack carried her forward and she rolled, hand still clutching desperately to the sword embedded in the soldier's spine.

His blood covered the floor, a flood of red as his life quickly drained from him. She tugged at the blade, but it was firmly lodged in his spine.

The other guard rounded on her, his surprise gone,

steel clutched in his fist. She jerked at the sword, but it remained firmly stuck in his spine.

"You ought to have stayed in your cell."

She glared up at the soldier. He had blood on his tired face, and there was still a trace of fear in his brown eyes. Kritcha released the sword. She kicked the soldier whose nose she had broken, making sure that she wouldn't get any surprises from behind.

"Let me go, and I won't have to hurt you. I just want to get out of here."

He scoffed, his bulbous nose scrunched up in disgust.

"You ain't goin' nowhere, lousy whelp."

He lunged at her, but she was ready. She ducked to the side. His blade hit the stone wall behind her, and she kicked at him with all the force she could muster. Already off balance from the missed blow, he fell against the wall, his head hitting the stone with a hard crack.

"You little bitch!"

He swung around, contacting the air where her head had been only seconds before.

Off balance again, her blow forced him back against the wall.

"I'll kill you, you cunt!"

He was panting. His face a fiery red. Blood ran from his temple where he had struck the wall. It mingled indiscriminately with the blood of his dead partner.

He swung again, but his own blood had blinded him. His blows fell nowhere near their mark.

Kritcha crouched on the back of the soldier with her blade in his neck. With both hands on the hilt she shook the blade violently back and forth while pulling up trying to free it.

"I'll get you!" The soldier swung wildly, blinded by the blood in his eyes. She hoped beyond hope that he wouldn't find her by chance before she had freed the short sword from his friend's neck.

With all her weight she pulled back and the blade gave a little. Redoubling her efforts, she gave another pull. She heard something snap, perhaps more of his spine breaking; there was a gurgle, maybe the last bit of air escaping from the soldier's lungs. She didn't know. She didn't care; it was almost free. She gave one more exhaustive tug on the sword. Finally, with a dull thud the blade was free. The soldier's head was barely connected to his shoulders by a thin string of sinew. It rolled lazily to one side, blue eyes staring off into nothing.

"Bitch!" He had stopped swinging and wiped his eyes.

"There you are!" But it wasn't the guard's voice.

The Lord of Green Boughs dashed around the corner. One of the soldiers still with him.

"Stop her!" Green Boughs cried, and the soldier turned to see who was shouting. Distracted by the shout, Kritcha quickly stuck her newly freed blade through the soldier's neck. His cry turned to a wet gargle as blood poured into his mouth.

Stooping, she liberated the soldier she had stabbed of his sword and moved quickly down the corridor.

"Where are you going? There is no way that you can escape!" The Lord of Green Boughs shouted to her.

She didn't care. She would find a way.

CHAPTER ELEVEN

Kritcha kept running. She pushed herself beyond what she thought was possible, beyond what her mind could possibly endure. It had been a long few days, exactly how many had passed she couldn't be sure. One thing she did know for sure was that she wouldn't be able to take much more. Especially if she didn't find something to eat.

The corridors and passages all ran together. Endless winding ways of cut stone and wooden doors. Occasionally there were stairs, some that went up, some that went down. She never followed the ones that went down. Her logic being that she didn't know where she was going, but that for the sake of consistency and her own sanity she would go up, because in her mind up meant out and that was enough to keep her going. At least for the time being.

She paused for a second at an intersection. Taking several deep breaths, she tried to calm herself a little, to clear her head and think for a second. In the distance she heard shouts. She didn't have long to think.

Something else caught her attention. Was it? She sniffed the air, her stomach let out a low, sonorous growl. Food. She couldn't tell what exactly, but to her, at this point, it didn't matter. Her stomach let out another growl, and like a hound on a ham, she followed her nose. First down a set of stairs then through several wider chambers. Possibly old dining halls? She didn't know. She didn't care, her stomach had taken over.

Kritcha heard voices ahead. She paused to listen, to see what exactly it was they were doing.

"You trust 'im?" asked a man.

"Who?" asked a second voice. A rough-sounding woman's.

"This Lord of Green Boughs. The way 'e keeps bringin' southerners up here and that Strand fellow, what's 'is deal thinkin' 'e can boss us around."

"Don't really care to be honest. As long as 'e keeps paying me, I'll keep cookin' 'is meals and keep my 'ead down, maybe it won't get chopped off in some fools' war."

"Who said anythin' about a war?" asked the first with a grunt.

Kritcha kept moving closer. The smell of hot food

flooded into her nostrils. Onions and carrots, beef and potatoes. Warm bread. Her stomach growled so loudly she thought the two might hear it. She put her index finger to her lips to quiet her stomach, but then realized how crazy that was. She shook her head and continued forward. She really needed food.

"Yeah, ain't you 'eard? Once we find this woman, this Idiri, they want us to march south," said the woman.

The man scoffed, "Nothin' good down south, bunch a tarts and twats is all they are. They can keep their crazy queen."

The woman laughed, "I 'ear she once killed an entire village because they wouldn't give up a girl that she 'ad a fancy on."

"A girl? See nothin' but tarts down there, the lot of 'em."

"Naw, it ain't like that. See, she takes them and makes them into her consort of sorts and then she steals the youth from them, sucks the life right out of 'em. She only takes the prettiest ones though; she's some kind of Faytall they say. They say she never ages. That she's going to live forever."

Kritcha could see the pair now. They were working in a steam-filled room with five stone ovens along one wall, fires glowing in all but one of them. Over an open fire a huge cauldron simmered. The woman stirred it and lifted the ladle to her lips, thick brown gravy of a hearty stew dripped to the floor.

Kritcha licked her own lips, and her stomach growled again.

"The Faytall ain't no joke; my ol' Pa said he met one once."

"Well, then your ol' Pa is full of shit; ain't no man survived to speak of the Faytall."

"'e did too. Said 'e was too ugly and mean for 'er."

The woman bent double laughing, "Guess we know where you get your looks from then."

The man turned to her and scowled, "You just watch your stew."

He turned and inspected one of the ovens. With a rough toss he threw logs into a couple of their fires. The woman was still laughing.

"Did I 'urt your feelings? You ain't that ugly. I'm sure some Faytall would scoop you up in a 'eart-beat."

He just shook his head.

Kritcha crawled on her belly toward the door of the kitchen. There was a rack near the entrance where they had bread left to cool and pies—hopefully minced-meat, those were her favorite. Another growl from her stomach compelled her forward.

She slid up to the wooden shelves, slithering like a snake about to catch its prey, but instead of a mouse it was a minced-meat pie. She slowly removed one of the morsels from its place on the shelf, her predicament forgotten for the moment, her only focus the food she held in her hands.

She devoured the pie, ripping into it like a bear in a

bee-hive, only thankfully without the stinging bees. Bits of pastry flew from her mouth covering her hands and face as she demolished the tasty pie.

"'ey what you doin' over there?"

Kritcha didn't notice that the woman had stopped stirring her stew. She didn't notice the raised ladled that swung down and like a club bludgeoned her on the head, spattering Kritcha with hot gravy and other bits from the stew.

"What you think yer doin' eating one of my pies like a feral forest child."

Kritcha's eyes went wide, and she almost dropped the pie. Almost.

"You put that back and get out of 'ere; this food ain't fer you."

Kritcha started eating faster. She dodged another swing of the ladle, maintaining control of her pie she rolled to the left out and away from the woman.

"I didn't say eat faster! Gimme that pie!" the woman came at her again ladle swinging.

"What's all yer fuss about over here, Jorin?"

The man asked sauntering over a small axe in his hand.

"Get it, Smit! It's got one of yer pies!"

"Shit, where'd it come from?" yelled Smit.

"I don't know, does it matter?"

Smit raised his axe and Jorin her ladle, and they both advanced on Kritcha.

"Come on now, don't be afraid. We ain't goin' to 'urt

you," said Smit in a soothing voice, intended to belay a sense of safety. Kritcha most certainly did not feel safe. She continued to eat the pie, which she had almost half finished.

Jorin snorted, "We most certainly will 'arm you if you don't stop eatin' that pie."

"Shut up, you'll scare 'er if you keep on like that."

"I don't care, we just got to get 'er out of 'ere."

The ladle came at Kritcha again, and she dodged it once more. Just as she recovered from the missed blow, she heard something. Footsteps? Hurried footsteps... they were close too. The food and the cooks had distracted her; now she really had to hurry. She would have to eat the pie on the run. She raised herself up, not letting go of her grip on the pie.

"'ey, where do you think you're going?"

There were shouts from behind her down the passages where she had come from.

"Do you see her?" the Lord of Green Boughs asked. He sounded out of breath.

She threw the pie in the face of the Jorin, and the woman recoiled trying to brush bits of pie from her face. Smit swung his axe, but his swing met with air, and she was gone.

CHAPTER TWELVE

Kritcha moved quickly, but she wasn't quick enough. A hand grasped at her ankle and pulled her down. A soldier she hadn't seen, from a doorway she hadn't noticed. She caught herself into a roll and tried to carry her momentum forward. But another soldier was there to catch her, and he tried to pin her down. She kicked and squirmed, wiggling free of his grasp. The first soldier dove after her, but this time he just missed her ankle. She ran headlong into a darkened corridor off one of what Kritcha had presumed to be old dining halls.

Shouts and the heavy foot-falls of soldiers clad in iron-shod boots followed closely on her heals. Desperation drove her on, as she bounced off walls in the darkened passage. She was blind, but so were they. She slowed her pace to a fast walk, keeping her hands outstretched in front of her to keep from running face-first into the walls she couldn't see.

Besides the walls she felt something else. Something that pulled at her, mind, body and spirit. The passage was dark, but that wasn't it. It was the strange feeling like when she had been near to the Lord of Green Boughs. Only this was deeper, more visceral. A primal sensation. One as old as the earth itself.

It was strange, the feeling, like a fog that fell about her mind, shrouding her thoughts. It was a hopelessness unlike any she had ever felt before. She wanted to stop, to slump down, right there in the hallway even with the heavy footfalls of the soldiers closing in on her.

She wondered what the point of it was. Running. They would just find her again. They would just keep coming. Why did it matter?

The footsteps behind her slowed from a run into the slow rhythm of a careful walk. What was this place? Her eyes felt heavy, as though she might soon fall asleep. There was a shout from behind her. It startled her, but she still didn't move any faster.

"Get after her!" It was the Lord of Green Boughs. She recognized the voice.

There was a glow behind her. She turned her head; its weight was so great now. It was as though she were carrying a boulder on her neck; her movements felt slowed and heavy. She waved her hand in front of her face; it felt like she was moving underwater, like time itself had slowed.

Kritcha watched as the torch drew near. She closed her eyes, and the radiant warmth of its yellow light filled her mind. A hand grabbed her. She just wanted to sleep. To rest. How many days had she been running? Under the ground there were no days, or weeks, or seasons to pass. There was only darkness. There was only hopelessness.

The hand was shaking her. She didn't care. There was a face, but cast in the deepest shadow. A black so dark it swallowed all light. Its lips moved mouthing words to her, but she couldn't hear them, or couldn't understand them, she wasn't sure which. There was a blinding light, and she opened her eyes.

The Lord of Green Boughs was inches from her face. His once pale and calm face had gone flush, his hair was mussed. His lump shook. It brushed against her and she shivered, a chill ran through her.

A look of confusion crossed the forest lords face. He glanced down at his chest.

"What have you seen?"

Kritcha closed her eyes again, but there was only black. There was no light. It was an abyss.

"A face..."

"Whose face? Tell me what you have seen."

Kritcha shook her head, "I don't know what it was. It spoke but I couldn't hear what it was saying. It was cast in shadow. I—"

Concern crossed the forest Lords face.

"Who was it?"

She shook her head.

"Get her up."

The guards lifted her from the ground, she didn't remember falling. Her hands hurt though, like they had touched something extremely hot. She wanted to sleep, her body ached, she needed to rest.

She closed her eyes again, her head was clearing, at least a little. The darkness and despair had faded, if only slightly. One guard was holding her under her arms and dragging her further down the darkened corridor. The Lord of Green Boughs was leading the way. The torch in his hand.

They passed countless corridors, blackened maws yawned open at them, their inky dark waiting to swallow her up. She wanted so badly to sleep, to rest. The soldier walking behind her blinked slowly. His eyes looked heavy too, what was happening to them?

For a moment there was a flash, like a comet that burned across her mind. Something old, like hope. Something familiar, like courage sprang back into her body. Kritcha launched herself into the soldier walking behind them. She pushed her head straight into his stomach. They both rolled into a heap on the floor.

The one that had been carrying her joined onto the pile, and there was a scrum as they all three fought to get the upper hand. She punched and kicked, breaking jaws and noses as she did. She bit whatever she could find, fingers, hands, ears, anything. One of the soldiers howled in pain as she removed his ear from the side of his head. She tasted his blood in her mouth.

"Enough!" The Lord of Green Boughs shouted above the din.

"What hope do you yet retain that you still fight to be free?"

The three stopped their fight, and Kritcha met his gaze. Her eyes narrowed, blood running down her chin, the soldiers ear gripped firmly in her teeth.

She spat the ear out onto the ground to answer the lord. "I have the only hope I have ever had. And that is that I can survive, that I will make it out of this place and that I will be free from you."

The soldiers weren't holding her. One held the side of his head, blood seeping through his fingers. The other was on his hands and knees behind them. Only the lord opposed her now.

His lips pursed, and his eyes narrowed, "You have no hope."

With one great burst of energy and fury, she stole a sword from the guard nearest her and barreled into the Lord of Green Boughs. The blow appeared to catch him, completely by surprise because he made no effort to stop her. Only to call out to her as she ran, into the dark that waited to consume her.

"There is no escape for you, Kritcha!"

CHAPTER THIRTEEN

She went on for a time, careening off walls in the dark of the ancient forest palace. She went until she saw something. The faintest trace of light. Her heart leapt at the thought. If there was light, there might be a way out. She broke into a run, heart pounding.

The chamber was darkened save for a single shaft of sunlight that cut through and like a knife stabbed into the darkness. At the bottom was a raised dais upon which sat a pedestal, with what looked like a bowl at its top. Curiosity got the better of Kritcha, and for the moment, danger forgotten, she focused on the strange thing in front of her.

She walked slowly up to it. She held her hand into the light. The sun's warmth felt good on her tired skin. It was something she hadn't seen for what felt like months. She put both hands into the light turning them over. Inspecting them.

There was blood and the remnants of the purloined pie she had been forced to use as a weapon. Old scars covered them, scars that she had earned in years of surviving. Each told a story. Each held a memory.

She felt her side where the Laroo's claw had penetrated her. There were many new lines that had been added to the story in the last few days.

Kritcha looked back into the water. It looked deep. Far deeper than it deserved to be. She touched the bottom of the bowl just to be sure that it only went that far down.

She looked back into the dark water. Her weary face peered back, matted hair ringed in a halo of golden sunlight.

She wanted to touch the water, to use it to cleanse her battered face. But there was something about it, something that made her hesitate, something that held her hand. She stuck her sword through her belt; hopefully there it would be safe.

Kritcha moved her face closer to the bowl her nose mere inches from the surface of its water. An air of calm radiated from its surface. She reached her hands up and splashed the cold water over her face.

A wave-like darkness washed over her and she was thrown back from the bowl and its cold water. Hopelessness pervaded her mind once more.

"Do you feel it? The hopelessness? The emptiness?" Kritcha shook her head and turned to see the Lord of Green Boughs walking slowly toward her through the darkened chamber. "The greatest weapon in war is not a sword or a knife. It is hopelessness, the hopelessness that comes with defeat. Break their spirit and rip from their chests their still-beating hearts, and they will no longer have the strength to oppose you. Shattered minds do not good soldiers make. You may break a million bodies and cast their bones to the wolves, but if their minds are keen they will oppose you. Victory cannot be attained by the sword; it must come from a broken mind. Break the mind, then you have won a victory from which there can be no return. I see I have yet to break your mind. It too will fall, in time I will wear it down."

She tried to roll over to push herself up, but she was met with a fierce and angry pain in her arms and legs.

"I will wash clean all pestilence and bring a new age upon the earth. One golden. One bright and beautiful. I will begin with the Queen of White Lilies and what strength still lies within that hollow chest. I have heard it said that if you seek revenge you should dig two graves." His face was cast in shadow; the torch must have gone out when she attacked him. "I shall dig ten thousand and lay bare the folly of a queen obsessed with the dead."

"What do you need me for then? Why do you need any of us?" She felt down where the sword had been, but it was gone. She glanced around quickly. Where was it?

He smiled at her and knelt next to her. He dipped his finger into the blood that was running down her face from her temple, where her head had struck the floor.

"This." He rubbed her blood between his fingers. "This is old; in it lies a power that has long since vanished from the world. The power to create and the power to destroy. The power to heal and the power to bring back what was lost so long ago. If she will not come then maybe..."

His eyes took on a distant quality as he absently rubbed his fingers together.

"If what you need is our blood, then why do you need my mother at all? You already have so much of it?"

"Because Idiri is the only one that remains that can make the pure weld, because she can take whatever spell her and her kind used to keep the Laroo out of the waters' hold and get rid of it. I do not know where the Queen of White Lilies found her own source of the pure weld. Perhaps Idiri favors her over us."

His last was more statement than a question to her.

"What matter is it if she favors anyone?"

His eyes focused back on Kritcha, "She should not

meddle in our affairs, Idiri, was sworn to protect, to heal, to remove all pestilence from the world. But I believe she has forgotten the promise she made, the promise only to heal and if she has given that strength to the white Lily then she has broken that oath. I believed I could force her to help me, as she surely must have helped the White Lily. Force her to use what she knows for a higher purpose, for a better purpose than just *healing.*"

"What oath would she have taken that would prevent her from giving such help to anyone?" Kritcha asked trying to sit up. Her head spun. She just wanted to sleep, to curl up into a ball and gently weep herself into a calm, everlasting sleep.

"Has she forgotten why it was she healed at all? Has she forgotten her old strength? Forgotten, what she could be—what we could be...if only she would come to me now. Then nothing would stand..."

He glared down at Kritcha, "If only she would reveal herself, if only she would help, then... then we would be strong enough. That is why I need *you.* That is why I need her."

"Why would she come? If she favors no side? Why help you or any of us."

"Idiri, watches all of her many children, if only ever from a distance, but she is there. Always. In her many forms she is watching. Sometimes the shade, sometimes the great gray eagle, sometimes the woman still young of face but old of heart and spirit. She is always watching and biding what time she has been given by the weld."

He rolled her over onto her back. She winced as another wave of pitch-black dark washed over her, and pain like fire enveloped her body.

"You see what I have has been diluted. The blood that my siblings and I took was not the pure weld. That is why I need her, your mother, to give me the pure weld, the old blood, it is a secret that only she knows. There were others, but time has taken them, if I could have made it any other way I would have. But it is said that the purer the blood the deeper the madness. I haven't seen any such side effect yet."

Kritcha pushed herself away from the forest lord as best as she could against the pain.

"Why would you take it then?"

He moved a little closer to her. His face only inches from her own.

"It was her idea, the Queen of White Lilies, Mordina Semberlund. We all took it—my nine brothers and sisters and I and her. I didn't know it then, but it was her way of trying to control us. She made us do it. A stupid dare, but the promise of immortality..." he sucked in through his teeth and closed his eyes. "That can sway even the strongest hearts." He looked back down at her. "We had heard the legends. We knew the danger, but we wanted to outlive her. She took it first, before we had time to think. She believed that by forcing the weld onto us she could make us submit, that the madness would take us, and she could claim the throne for herself without trouble. That she could control her own madness, but the old blood is strong. Now she spends her time, pining for the brother she never met. Ignorant, as her domain slowly crumbles, and danger grows on every border, waiting to carve up what she has neglected. I wouldn't have neglected my mother's realm. What it is now is nothing to what it was."

Kritcha twisted away from the Lord of Green Boughs.

"But she was wrong. We did not submit, and our mother's throne was not so easily stolen."

He looked hungry now, a lust born of long years spent filled with burning desire. His teeth were bared. In the glow of the room he looked like a demon, eyes of fire and hatred.

"It is an effect of the weld. The madness that comes of the mind of those who are not born with the blood. She called us all to the keep after her father had died. We didn't know what she wanted. When she came at my oldest brother, Drendel, we were all taken by surprise. The next two eldest went after her, but the weld blood had given her strength that even the two of them could not match. She had found some of the old blood; she had found the real power of the ancient world. That is the power that I seek from your mother. I seek only the strength to take back what is rightfully ours. To restore an empire once the glory of the continent, an empire that your mother had a hand in breaking."

He leaned in and touched Kritcha, brushing her hair back from her face. She shuddered at the touch. It was cold, the fingers clammy, more like a corpse than a man. She recoiled from the Lord of Green Boughs. His eyes narrowed at her, the smile vanished from his lips, the thin things becoming a line pressed hard together.

"They say that I have the madness too."

"You said that she broke an empire, but there have been no empires on this continent."

"There was once. But she used it, your mother. She used it to fight Yeriret. She took its people and its blood and its wealth and sent it all away to the north where they were drained."

He reached for her again. She pushed herself up off the floor and away from the man. The thin line of his pursed lips dipped down into a scowl.

"There is no use in running from me there is no escape from what you are. We will find you again and again and again..."

His eyes drifted into the distance staring past her into the darkness of the chamber. She scooted back further, and he shook his head, eyes focusing back on her.

There was a strange fire that smoldered within his eyes. Something that terrified her, because it was something that she didn't fully understand, because it was something that felt strangely familiar. It was as though she had felt it before, as though she had seen that fire burning in the eyes of others.

What madness was this that drove him? If it was in the blood…did she have it too? What was it he had said about those born with it?

"Do not be frightened of me. We are after all of a kind, you and I. We both have the blood of the ancients flowing within us; let me show you."

With his left hand he reached under his robe. The lump at the center of his chest twitched and wiggled. He pulled a long knife from the folds of his black robe.

"Let us see how we are the same."

He came at her a hungry look in his now-fiery eyes.

"Let us, let our blood mingle as it did of old. Let us let it dance upon the stones and drown the world in its power. Watch it flow over the world and make it clean, make it pure. A sacrifice upon the altar of despair!"

Kritcha scooted away from him. She found her sword that had been flung away when she had touched the altar. She picked it up and pointed it at the advancing Lord of Green Boughs.

"I will kill you."

"I know." His voice was flat and matter of fact. "I will give you the very same courtesy when the time comes."

"I thought you needed us?"

"I do, but it would seem your mother is less protective and caring for her children than I initially thought. I believe it's time to try a heavier hand."

He lunged at her, but she was ready for the strike and propelled herself back and up from the floor. His knife met with the stone where she had been sitting only moments before.

"We found many of you, but she was careful to hide her children well. I have been looking for them for a very long time. I do not know what her intention was with all of you. So many up here, why?"

A brief look of consternation crossed his face.

"What does she want up here that she would place so many of her children here?"

Kritcha didn't know if he wanted an answer or if he was merely thinking out loud to himself. Either way she, for the moment, didn't care about the answer. That wasn't to say she didn't eventually want to know what it all meant, but for the time being she would be satisfied to escape with her life. Before the Lord of Green Boughs was given the chance to let their blood *mingle* upon the altar. She shuddered at the thought of it.

"Do you know how many brothers and sisters you have?"

Kritcha shook her head, keeping her eyes on him while trying to find some way that she might escape from the dark chamber. Some hole or tunnel that led out of there, but he stood between her and the only exit that she knew of.

"I've found at least twenty of you. I have managed to capture eight; the rest will soon fall into place though. Then I can move south. Then I can restore what was lost."

He lunged at her again. What she could see of his face looked hungry. Maybe even desperate. He was crazy, if it was in the blood...

Then it flowed through her veins too.

She dodged the strike, her mind focused on the door that she knew lay somewhere in the dark just behind the forest lord's back.

The hopelessness she noticed seemed to lessen as she drew further from the altar at the center of the chamber. As hope grew the fire in her body grew, her desire to live grew. She had to get out of this place, and she had to do it quickly.

"Your eyes are not your friends; they are mine." The Lord of Green Boughs backed away from her toward where she knew the door had to be.

"You want to escape." He shook his head, the scowl on the thin line of his lips deepened. "But there is no escape; you must get through me first."

She didn't follow the forest lord. Her eyes flitted about the room searching for any other way out than past him. The footsteps of soldiers in heavy boots echoed about the room.

Her desperate eyes met with the shaft of sunlight. It was desperate, it was crazy, but it just might be her only chance. She secured her appropriated short sword in the stolen belt and went to the base of the wall nearest where the sunlight entered the chamber.

The soldiers were getting closer. She ran her hands over the cut stone wall. It was smooth, but time and neglect had eaten at the masonry and like a baby with an apple left it pocked with holes. Not deep, just enough to fit in fingers and toes.

She reached up as high as she could in the dark hoping to find a hold; if she could get high enough before they reached her she knew they wouldn't be able to climb the wall in their heavy boots and armor.

"You really are crazy aren't you? That you think you get out of here past us." The Lord of Green Bough's voice was mocking, "Go ahead, try, and we'll scrap your corpse from the floor when you have fallen to your death."

Kritcha ignored his mocking voice. She would try and they wouldn't be scraping her up off the floor she was going to make it. She had to.

Desperate seconds crawled on as she tried to find a hold good enough to pull herself up. The soldiers pace quickened as they drew nearer to her away from the altar. Steel glinted briefly in the sun-light.

Her fingers gripped at wet stone and she pulled herself up, toes digging into the highest holds they could find. With her free hand she began searching for another hold to pull herself up further.

"You won't get out that way. The hole is too small, even for you."

A hand swiped at her ankle, but she found a hold and pulled herself up just in time to avoid it. Out of reach but far from being out of danger she kept going, the soldiers following her progress as she crawled like a giant spider up the domed ceiling toward the hole. And freedom.

A few times she slipped, her feet dangling almost within reach of the soldier's hands or swords. The Lord of Green Boughs laughed each time she did, hoping for her failure. She was delighted to disappoint him.

The sun on her face felt better than any other time she had ever felt it before. Its warmth gave her strength, gave her hope. She pulled herself around the lip of the shaft and into the light. She heard the shuffle of feet below and the sound of voices. She couldn't tell what they were saying, she didn't care. She was almost free.

Kritcha shinnied up the narrow shaft, some of the sharper rocks digging into her sides and stomach. Her already-tattered clothing was going to pieces. Soon, she thought, there would be nothing left, and she'd be running around stark-raving naked. But if she made it out of this wretched place that didn't matter. Her life mattered more to her than her modesty. She kept going up, the light of the sun giving her a strength she hadn't felt since she had been captured. She pushed harder, knowing that she was so close to the outside and what she hoped would be freedom.

She could smell fresh air. Clean air. The air of the forest, filled with leaves and trees, the sounds of birds filtered down to her. She moved faster, the scant food she had gotten giving her new strength to push forward.

The light was blinding, but it felt good. The warmth of the sun on her face after so long in the dark, dank tunnels of Ostenae-Bar.

She rolled out of the shaft on the forest floor, as though she had been spit from the earth. Apparently, it didn't like the taste of her. Had chewed on her for a bit, and then let her go. She looked down at her body; it really did look like she had been chewed on. Her clothes were in tatters, shredded from the trip in the river and the climb up the shaft. Dried blood covered her arms and face, hands and body. Luckily most of it wasn't hers. She prodded her side where the Laroo claws had penetrated her; it was sore to be sure, but the poison of the dart had wanted her all to itself, so it had kept her blood from souring and raising her to a fever.

Kritcha stood on shaking legs and walking slowly forward she scanned the surrounding forest. There was nothing, no shouts from hurried men trying to catch her, no horrid calls from the nasty Laroo. She stopped for a moment, leaning against what she thought was a natural rock formation. She felt the stone, but it was strange, it felt like...No, it couldn't be... A heartbeat.

She took a step back and for a second could swear that the ancient moss-covered statue had black pupilless eyes that stared out at her. It was only a second then they vanished, and there was nothing save the ancient stone. A broken arm that might have once held a spear or sword and one that still held a shield.

Then she heard the shouts and the hurried footsteps of men in pursuit. And she swore that there was, if only for a second the smallest hint of a smile on the statue's ancient lips.

CHAPTER FOURTEEN

S ten pulled himself up onto the jagged rocks that surrounded the pool. The Hopper was nowhere to be seen. He felt his side. Blood oozed from a gash there. Not deep or long, enough to hurt, enough to catch a fever and sour his blood.

The longer he sat there, he realized that he was covered with cuts. His clothes were shredded, and his neck throbbed. It hurt to swallow. He had to fight for each breath.

He had come out of the dark of the caves to be deposited in a deep pool surrounded on all sides by ancient pine and cedar trees. Soaked from head to toe in the frigid water of the river, he shivered and took a long, slow breath. It was hell to swallow; each time it brought memories of Durdar's gift. He stroked his throat; even light touches felt like needles being stuck into his skin. He pushed the breath out and closed his eyes. His feet still dangled in the water. Caught in an eddy the foam was turning red from his blood. He watched it for a moment. Mesmerized by the simple motion.

Sten's head drooped, heavy with the effort of wrestling the big Hopper. He hadn't eaten in days. At least not anything good or substantial.

He closed his eyes and took another deep breath. There was a splash. Something big.

Sten's eyes opened in an instant. He tried to pull his feet up, but something held them. Through the red foam a shape emerged. An empty socket. One dark malicious eye. A grin filled with razor teeth. The smooth domed head of the Hopper.

Sten struck the brute. Hard. In its good eye. It howled, releasing Sten's feet. He pushed himself up out of the water and scrambled backward over the jagged rocks that surrounded the pool; he had to stay out of the water. The thing would be tough enough to fight without steel on land, but if they went back into the water, Sten knew he would lose. The only thing that had kept him alive was the current. The river had done more work than he had to fight off the big Hopper. In the calmer waters, he wouldn't stand a chance against the thing.

It was slippery and nimble. The water was its home. Sten continued to back away from the water. The thing slowly rising out of it still smiling. It lunged after his feet. He pulled them away just in time, and the brute was thrown off balance.

"Warm blood! Warm blood! *Gitcha, Gitcha.*"

Sten kicked out with both feet, catching the thing full in the face. With a splash and a curse in some Hopper language, the thing fell back into the water.

Sten turned from the pool, making to run from the thing, but as he did he caught the flash of something quick. Little more than a blur between the branches. Was it the woman? Had she made it too?

He started off after the thing. Which took some great effort—his whole body ached, stiff and sore from the icy water and the beating it had taken against the rocks.

"Warm blood! Warm blood!"

Gitcha, Gitcha, Gitcha, Gitcha-a-Laroo!

The chorus was taken up by what sounded to be a hundred other Hoppers. They were everywhere. Branches snapped all around him. The sun was setting; it would be dark soon. Making his flight that much more difficult. He couldn't see the woman anymore. He wanted to find her, but right now had to get out of this place, away from the Hoppers.

He moved as fast as he dared with the net of the Hoppers tightening about him.

KRITCHA DARTED from tree to tree. Catching branches in her face and stomach. Her body burned where they caught and cut her, leaving small scrapes over everything.

A cry went up all around her.

Gitcha, Gitcha, Gitcha, Gitcha-a-Laroo!

It was so loud and sounded so close she thought that they were in the trees with her. She turned, expecting to see one there. How it would be moving after her she couldn't have said, but she expected it nonetheless.

When she turned her head, she missed the next branch. Her hands shot out groping for it, but it was too late; they found only air and then her body found the earth.

She didn't move. She didn't know if she could. She dug her hands into the dead leaves that covered the ground. The earth felt good, almost comforting.

She could hear them. Blundering through the forest all around her. She wondered when they would see her.

"Do you think you can escape? Did you think that I would let you?"

Was it Green Boughs speaking? Maybe. She couldn't be sure.

"You're a very strong woman. Stronger than the others." She could see his feet standing near to her. "But you've had a much harder life than they have." He squatted next to her.

"Your mother put the rest in more..." he reached

down and rolled her over. "Important, or rather, more comfortable positions. Replacing the children of nobility or wealthy northern merchants. She wanted her own blood to drown out all the rest in the north. It is only my blood that stood between her and that end, mine and that of my siblings."

Kritcha's head was swimming, not only from the fall but from what he was saying.

"Replaced?" was all that she could manage.

"You don't know what you are, do you?" he brushed her hair back from her face. "Womb thief, unborn killer, red morning child. There was a time when your mothers would place you in the soil and you would grow."

Kritcha dug her hands in deeper. She had fistfuls of leaves now. He kept talking.

"Like any other seed their eggs would pull nutrients from the soil and would take on the characteristics of that place, green hair and eyes, pale skin and long slender bodies like the trees that shared the soil. But those caches were a delicacy to the Laroo, so the mothers took to hiding them in ever more devious places. But then they had a better idea, a sick and malicious idea. They took up their eggs, and while the pregnant human mothers slept they would place their own eggs inside of them. And then a battle would begin, one new life against another. The intruder is bigger. The intruder is stronger. So it forces the natural child out."

He lifted her head up. His hands were cold. Clammy even. Why wasn't he sweating? His face was flushed, but he wasn't sweating. He was barely even breathing hard. She was drenched, or maybe it was water from her trip down the river. She couldn't tell any more.

"I could kill before I could even walk or talk or think," she said. Her body throbbed from the fall and the exertion of the flight from the cells.

"Yes, you and all your kind are natural killers, hence red morning child, because a woman shouldn't bleed after she conceives, her visits from Clessid should end at conception. But you pushed the other out, because you have to in order to survive, and it is that process that makes the red morning."

He looked around; the forest had gone silent. The Laroo had moved on.

Kritcha pulled her head from his hand. He stood and walked around her.

"Only Idiri can let the Laroo into the water's hold, only she can give to me, the broken line of Errander-more, the strength I need to destroy the Queen of White Lilies. She can give to me the old weld, she can make me stronger, she can make the Laroo stronger. The Laroo are strong but all that strength comes from north of Vulfeermus-Nigh, I need a hold closer to the White Lily. So I took you and all the others that I knew of in the north to threaten your real mother's own plan, whatever that may have been, to draw her out, to make her more pliable to my ends."

"But my mother didn't come, did she? She didn't oblige you." Kritcha, closed her eyes tightly. The darkness felt good.

"She is here..." he paused, Kritcha opened her eyes. "She is always near. She is always watching all of you..."

He looked around as though he might catch a glimpse of her through the trees.

Kritcha sat up. She didn't know how much more she could take. Her body was a pulp. Bloodied almost beyond use. She needed it to hold on just a little longer, just a little more to be rid of him.

She heaved a sigh and listened. The forest was silent.

"How do you know she can break the spell or whatever it is on the waters' hold to keep the Laroo out?" she asked, feeling for the sword she hoped was still in her belt.

"She was the oldest of the sixteen, and besides Yeriret, the strongest. When they built the waters' hold they used it to fight an ancient enemy, their only enemy, Yeriet, but whatever they did after kept the Laroo out. I'm going to let them in. And I will take the north from your true mother as I have taken her children, and then I'll take the south from White Lilies and the broken line of Errandermore will be restored." He was pacing and looking frantically about as though something might burst through the trees at any second and strike him down. If only he knew that she was going to strike him down first.

She swung out with the sword and jumped to her feet. Her steel didn't meet flesh, only the lord's own steel. He was quick. Unnaturally quick. She had fought quick before. She had fought slow before and strong and smart and stupid. The only ones that worried her were the highly trained fighters. The ones that could adapt to anything. That could predict any move before you even thought about it. Luckily, she hadn't met many of those in the north woods.

The Lord of Green Boughs was no expert. Trained to be sure. Trained very well. So his moves were practiced, ingrained in his mind and hands since birth, and that for her was her best defense. He would only know how to react in ways that he had been trained to, to attacks and maneuvers he had practiced himself, and she wouldn't indulge him that courtesy. Her attacks were wild, unpracticed, and unrefined; she hacked like a lumberjack at a tree, which worked better when she had a hatchet she knew. A sword would have to do for now.

Her only other advantage was her knowledge that she could endure more pain than her opponent could, under normal circumstances. These circumstances were far from normal. Her body wouldn't be able to take much, if any, more punishment. That meant she had to dodge better than she usually did.

She had always heard that sword-fighting was like

dancing. That the two opponents were locked in the beauty and majesty of combat. Kritcha knew that was a load of bear dung shoveled so high you could smell it a mile away.

It was brutal. It was death. There was no beauty in it. Especially when she was taking part. She had never learned to dance, but she could survive and that was exactly what she did.

He came at her. She threw off the blow intended for her stomach and kicked out, catching Green Boughs in the shin. He cursed and drew more steel; he held a short sword in each hand. His lump moving slightly with each attack.

He was dancing. Like lords and ladies and all the high and pompous knew how. She was fighting. She was fighting for her life.

"I thought you wanted us? I thought you needed us to find our mother?" she asked, dodging another blow.

"I needed you," he stepped back. "I thought that she would come and save you ragged lot of her own offspring, but it seems she doesn't care that much. So maybe if I kill enough of you she will come then."

He lunged at her. An excellent dancer. Too bad she wasn't. She sliced into his side, and he yelped in pain. He rolled through the leaves, springing back up before she could land a killing blow.

Green Boughs stood a few feet from her. He was painting his neat black robes torn and bloodied. His already-flushed face was even brighter red. Anger radiated out from his clenched teeth. She was frustrating him; that was even better—an angry opponent made more mistakes. The once-calm and collected forest lord had turned as feral as he had thought her to be. He must not do this often.

"If you're going to kill me, I really want to know. What is that?" Kritcha asked, pointing to his lump.

"This?" he asked, pointing towards it with his swords, "This, is a gift from the Queen of White Lilies." It began to move, wiggling like a snake caught under a blanket.

"I keep it because it would be far too painful to remove and because of my sister—"

The thing worked itself free from the tattered robes, twisting and writhing a slow path out of the black folds. A glint of steel and the thing was free. It was long and gangly like an arm made of pure sinew. It had patches of hair that didn't look human; the patches were too thick and long. The arm terminated in an awkward appendage, that seemed more a paw than a hand. It gripped the steel awkwardly, as though it couldn't hold it very well.

"Did you steal that from a bear?" Kritcha asked. Watching the thing twist and writhe about. Not unlike a cat's tail she thought. If it were malformed and nearly rotten.

"Mountain lion." he said, lunging at her again. All three appendages were raised. Swinging wildly. Almost madly about the lord as he advanced.

"Why take such a strange limb?"

"I didn't choose it." His blows were wild now. Desperate.

"Then why is it stuck to you? Why can't you control it?" Kritcha asked, defending as best she could against the ferocious onslaught.

"It was an accident. When we drank the blood. Took the old weld."

"Old weld? From Mordina Semberlund?"

But before she was able to ask more she realized she was slipping, falling backwards. She turned to see that their fight had brought them to the edge of the river. A cliff of at least thirty feet dropped away behind her. She was trapped.

"Another one of her brood dead. Idiri will not be pleased, but that was the point. She is the last. The only one that can stand against us or help us now." His voice was low, barely a growl. He glowered at her. A dark fire burning in his eyes. "The old alliances are dead. All those that took the allegiant gone. What can she do now but watch!" He came at her again.

She took the advance and used it to sweep him aside. As she did she caught the third arm about where she might call its elbow. The sinuous appendage writhed as the blade tore through flesh and bone. It was tougher than she thought it would be; she had to jerk upward on her sword several times to cut through. And with a crunch of bone she broke it free. The appendage flew wide, landing with a dull thud on the forest floor.

The Lord of Green Boughs howled. A strange, pinkish-colored liquid poured from the wound. He fell to the ground, dropping his swords and clutching his abdomen where the appendage had been. A stump remained from the limb and gushed the foamy pink liquid that should have been blood. Kritcha stopped for a moment. She was exhausted, she needed to rest, but there was no time for that now. She shook her head. Even the fire from the fight was leaving her.

She took a step closer to the lord but was halted before she could take another. She could see now that the lord was not just holding his stomach. He was holding the strange and severed limb up to the place where it had only moments before been attached.

Kritcha watched as the thing started to move again as the torn flesh reached out and covered the gap where her steel had broken it.

"What are you?" Kritcha asked, her mind trying desperately to comprehend what she was seeing. She failed miserably.

The lord smiled. His teeth were pink, and a froth was collecting at the corners of his lips.

"We are the healers of the world." He raised all three of his arms. "We that have the old blood."

Kritcha couldn't wait any longer. It didn't matter what he was, she couldn't fight him anymore. It had to end now. In two steps she was on top of him. She planted the heel of her foot squarely on his nose. He had reached for his swords, but she was too quick. The fire was back, if only for a moment.

He cried out as he fell. She didn't have time to watch him fall, only listen as he hit the water below. She had the more desperate job of pulling herself back up from over the edge.

When at last she was back on solid ground, she sat. Her body shook from head to toe. She could do nothing but sit; she wanted to sleep. She knew what she had to do. She was not safe here. Forcing herself up, she ran. Though she couldn't tell direction. Though she couldn't feel her legs nor taste the earth. She ran.

CHAPTER FIFTEEN

S ten stopped. The woods were quiet. Much too quiet for what he knew was following him. It had been three days since he had escaped Ostenea-Bar, and he had not stopped running. He had used a few old tricks he knew to throw them off his trail, but even then, it had only bought him a couple of hours. Precious hours to be sure—if he hadn't gotten them, he would have undoubtedly succumbed to exhaustion by now.

His blood pounded in his ears like great, ominous drums. His entire body ached from running for so long. Blisters covered his feet. His wounds were beginning to fester in the heat. He knew he had to be close to the waters' hold; they hadn't gone that far north, and even then, their progress had been slow. Unless he was going in circles, and if that were true, they should have caught him by now. He had to be close.

Something rustled in the leaves behind him. In the early morning, he still couldn't see clearly for the cover of the trees. He waited a moment. All he could hear was the drumming in his own ears. He squinted in the dark, trying to see the source. There was nothing.

He leaned back against a large tree. Closing his eyes for a second, he sat, taking long deep breathes, trying to slow his heart and clear his mind.

There it was again. The faintest rustle in the dark. His eyes were open, his heart pounding again. He bolted out into the dark, and as he did a chorus went up.

Gitcha, Gitcha, Gitcha, Gitcha-a-Laroo!

The voice of the big one followed.

"Hunt the hunt-man! Hunt the hunt-man!"

Sten ran on numb legs. His mind was blank, an empty mass of fear and fatigue. The lower branches of smaller trees whipped and tore at his already pulpy face. He didn't know what his goal was. The waters' hold? Maybe the camp of the southern armies? He didn't know. Fear gave him strength. It was the only thing still keeping him going.

He ran as fast as his legs would carry him. How could something that moved so slow when they had gone north move so fast now? Hatred gave them speed. It must for what else was there. He was nothing to them now.

He paused for a second. Gulping down as much air as his lungs would allow. They were still close; he could hear them blundering through the forest a couple hundred yards behind him.

Sunlight began to pierce the dense forest, stabbing through the thick green foliage with long yellow knives. Penetrating the gloom to which he had grown accustomed in the long hours since nightfall.

Something wasn't right here; over the clamor of the horde behind him he could hear something else. Footsteps, hurried and purposeful, soldiers. He turned to face the south. A glint of steel in the sunlight, Strand. It had to be.

Sten fell to his knees. The Hoppers were close now, almost on top of him. They would have him soon. He closed his eyes taking in a deep breath.

There was one behind him. He could smell it. It clicked its claws together.

Gitcha, Gitcha, Gitcha, Gitcha-a-Laroo!

There must have been a hundred of them. He opened his eyes. They were everywhere, a swarm of greenish brown, loping about in their froggish way.

He wondered why Strand was waiting? Why he hadn't broken his cover? Maybe he wanted revenge on the Hopper for the river. Maybe.

His thought was cut short by a thundering voice.

"Hunt-man, Hunt-man, warm blood fast, cold blood just as quick," Durdar said.

The others still milled about watching the forest and Sten. How hadn't they seen Strand?

"Where warm blood go now? No escape for the

warm blood, legs quick but not squirrelly-worrolly like old blood, find later cut out eyes, cut off squirrelly feet see how warm blood run then. Cut off hunt-man feet, see how he run without. Hunt-man make fine feast for Durdar. Warm cloak too."

A pair of the Hoppers grabbed Sten, hauling him up by the arms. He looked at the ugly things whose smell filled his nostrils. They were hideous things with bulbous eyes that protruded out and darted around watching everything.

They turned him around to face the big one, Durdar. They carried Sten forward, but he still couldn't see the brute. Sten let the creatures drag him through the dead leaves and sticks of the ancient forest. He didn't have the energy to fight anymore. If they wanted him so badly, they could have him.

The Hoppers that carried him stopped short. At first, Sten thought maybe they were waiting for the big one, but when he looked over at one of them he could see the reason they had stopped so suddenly. From the middle of its chest the Hopper was sporting an arrow. The head of which completely protruded from its greenish flesh. The other released its grip on his arm, the victim of a similar malady, the shaft and fletching protruding from its back. Strand.

There were a few moments in which the Hoppers, shocked at the suddenness of the attack, simply stood, their frog minds trying to process the new development. It didn't, however, take long for Sten's mind to process. He would have been gone in a flash if only he hadn't stopped for so long. His legs would no longer obey any commands they were given. He truly was at their mercy now.

A great cry rose from the trees all around them. Well-honed steel, polished to a mirror, shone out from the trees. It caught the sun's light, blinding all those careless gazes. It was thirsty, with a desire only blood could quench.

In an instant there were men everywhere. Their bright steel dancing in the morning's light. The bright swords quickly turned dark, as cold steel found cold blood and delighted to be fed such a feast of flesh. The Hoppers in their confusion scrambled over one another to be free from the harsh, ravenous desires of cold steel.

"Warm blood! Warm blood! Spill warm blood! Drink warm blood!" Durdar shouted above the din.

There were men around Sten now. Rough hands forced him up. Rough hands, but hands he noted that were mercifully devoid of claws.

"Form a line! They're coming back!" Men shouted around him.

"Who is this one?" a soldier asked. Sten was sure he pointed down at him, but he could barely keep his eyes open.

"One of the scouts. A favorite of the White Lily," said another.

"He's the one we've been looking for?"

"Better be," said a third soldier. "I can't stand these woods anymore—too many of these things up here." He kicked one of the Hoppers.

"Take him to Commander Crittondone. He'll want to see this one."

CHAPTER SIXTEEN

How many days passed, Sten couldn't tell. A week? A month? A full seasons turn? It could have been any of them or none. He honestly didn't know how long it had been, but it felt like ages. Rain pattered against the canvas top of the tent. It was dark inside and outside too, he guessed, since no light found its way in through the cracks in the corners of the tent. A single candle burned on a table next to him. It didn't help much in the damp gloom of the tent.

Sten tried to sit up but was met with overwhelming pain that emanated from every inch of his tired body. He lied back down, the cot groaning under his weight.

The flap on the tent opened, and a face poked in.

"He's awake," the soldier shouted back into the darkness. "Get the commander!" The face vanished behind the flap.

Sten listened to the rain falling. It was calming. His eyes drooped. Just as he started to drift off, the flap burst open and through it came the old commander, Crittondone.

"Well, look who's back in the realm of the living and the civilized." He stood over Sten, water dripping from his cloak and leather armor.

"Guess they didn't make a cloak of your hide after all. Eh, huntsman? Shame. I'm sure you would have made a fine cloak for that big fat Hopper."

"How did—"

Crittondone removed his hood.

"We can't leave until we have you," the commander smiled, a grim sardonic thing. "We've been looking for what I hoped would be a carcass. Maybe your face as part of one of those cloaks." Crittondone mimed a look of horror. His mouth open wide, eyes bulging.

"Then we could go home. Then we could tell the White Lily her prize pig was taken to slaughter," he motioned, and a stool was brought closer. Sten hadn't noticed the other soldiers. "But I should be so lucky." Crittondone sat with a deep sigh.

"What does she see in you, huntsman? All I've seen so far is failure. First you go and get you and ten of my soldiers caught—"

"They would have been better off if you had just—" Sten interjected, but Crittondone cut him off.

"Been better with you?" he laughed. "Look at you." Crittondone pulled Sten's blanket back.

"You look like something tried to eat you but didn't like the taste, so it spit you back out."

"It was your soldiers that—" Sten began but was cut off again.

"I don't care what excuses you have, huntsman. I'll get you to the White Lily, then she can deal with you."

"But I found her." Sten said, pulling his now-soggy blankets back over himself.

"Found who?" Crittondone asked, wringing water from his gloves.

"The one that escaped. From the village the Hoppers burned."

"What does that matter? She isn't my goal." The commander shook the water off his hands, smattering Sten with a cold shower. "You are, and tomorrow we are going south. Now that you're awake, you can travel, and we'll be leaving at first light."

"I have to find her. She knows what is going on up here!"

"We've been looking for your sorry carcass for over a week; the Hoppers have come twice in that time. We've had to move our camp because it would seem they are no longer afraid of the waters' hold. If you want to come back, you can. I am taking you to the White Lily, and we are leaving tomorrow. There will be no more discussion."

"You don't want to know what happened? Why they are moving south? I need to find her."

"And I need to get away from this Hopper-infested

place they call the north woods. No, I don't care about her. I don't care about you. I'm getting my men away from here as fast as possible." Crittondone stood, knocking the stool over.

"That's it then? All those lives for nothing?"

"Yes, it is, we have you and that's enough. We need an army up here. If I let you go find this woman...this Faytall, more will die," Critondone turned and walked to the door. "They killed almost half our men. I requested to leave, but we had to find you or at least your corpse, something that would match the crystalline assay."

"That's why I need to find her. She knows more about what's going on up here and this Lord of Green Boughs too. We have to find her!"

"We aren't doing anything but going south. I'll bring you to the White Lily if I have to tie you up and drag you there, *huntsman*."

"But—"

A scream pierced the night. Cutting through the patter of the rain against the roof of the tent.

"If that's them again!" Crittondone's voice boomed as he stormed from the tent.

"Everyone, to arms now! The Hoppers are back!" Sten heard Crittondone's voice fading.

He forced himself up. The pain gripped his entire body as though a giant hand were squeezing him, trying to wring the life from him as one might squeeze water from a sodden glove.

He was naked, and in the light of the candle, he could see some of his wounds. Red marks covered his body from head to toe. Most were just short marks, maybe an inch or two. There were a few, two or three running up his side, that were almost a foot long. Those had been crudely stitched and had already started to heal.

Another scream pierced the night, and he stopped his inspection. That wasn't a Hopper. He searched the tent for clothes. Pants, a shirt, hell, even an old sack would do. Anything to keep the rain off a little.

An old trunk in the corner seemed his best bet, no matter who it belonged to. Ratty pants and a tattered shirt were all that he found. They would have to do for now. He struggled into them and hobbled as best he could over to the entrance of the tent.

He pulled the flap back slowly, exposing the night beyond. Rain still fell steady and cold. It wasn't heavy, more of a mist that soaked through clothes and covered hair and skin. Enough to make him want to return to his tent and his cot. But curiosity had the better of him, so he kept going.

There was another scream. High and shrill in the night. A woman's scream. Could it be? Had she escaped the cell? Had she made it away from Ostenea-Bar?

Sten limped faster; each step was agony. He swore he could have pointed out each wound on his body with every footfall; it was like being stabbed in each of them all over again.

There was a large crowd of soldiers in the center of the camp. Some held torches. All looked on with swords drawn.

Another scream. The soldier nearest to Sten jumped a little. Sten pushed his way forward. Every bump and jostle stung his battered body. Several times he stubbed his bare feet on the soldiers' boots. He cursed each time. Occasionally the soldiers turned to look at him, eyes wide. Was it fear?

Sten broke through the ring. At its center stood Crittondone. His sword was drawn, and he was standing over a figure. Crittondone's back was toward him, his body obscuring the figure.

Whatever it was screamed again. The soldiers shifted nervously. Looking back and forth between each other and the figure.

Sten moved to go to the figure, but a hand arrested him. Clutching tightly at his arm.

"No, no, no, huntsman. The commander wants this one."

"But who?"

Crittondone turned, rain running down his face, tiny rivers in the torch light. He scowled, and his booming voice cut Sten off.

"Get back in your tent, huntsman. This doesn't concern you."

"Who is it?" Sten asked, struggling to be free from the soldier's grasp.

"It's nobody," said Crittondone. "Some feral woman... Faytall." He stepped back to reveal her.

"That's her! Kritcha!" Sten shouted trying even harder to be free. Another soldier grabbed his arm.

"It's who?" Crittondone asked, taking a step closer to Sten. "Did you screw her or something, huntsman?"

"She's the one they were after!" Sten stopped struggling. There was no use. He was too tired to fight them.

"Is that what you like, huntsman?" Crittondone raised his sword to point it at Sten. "You like crazy, wild women? Is that why you got caught?"

Sten looked past the commander at the woman. She did look crazy. Her eyes darted here and there. Her lips were moving as though she was speaking, only no sound passed them. She shook her head and closed her eyes. Another piercing scream, and her eyes were open, staring back at Sten. Almost like she recognized him. Then her eyes darted away.

Crittondone looked between them, lowering his sword.

"Let him go. Let's see if he'll give us a show."

The soldiers released their grip. Sten ran to her. Landing hard in the cold mud.

At first, she backed away. Scuttling like a crab, but when she saw the soldiers behind her, she stopped and stared at Sten.

"Why did they want you?" Sten asked; he didn't expect an answer.

He tried to make his voice as comforting as possible. He didn't know if it would work or not. Gone was the woman that had planned their escape. Sten wondered how long she had been running. How long it had been she had eaten or rested.

"Mother, mother, not my mother, mother, mother, not mine, but mine, mother!"

"Who is your mother?" Sten asked moving a little closer. Taking his time so not to spook her.

"Not my mother, not mine, someone else, other woman not mine, not mine."

Sten moved just a little closer.

"She needs food and rest." He said over his shoulder, hoping Crittondone would hear.

"And why would we give her that," he said walking up to her. "I wouldn't give her scraps. Feral woman, crazed Faytall, shouldn't even be alive." Crittondone raised his sword.

"Wait! You're just going to kill her?"

"What else should we do? Screw her? Like you did, taken in by this Faytall? By her wild charm? Must be like riding a bear."

"I didn't. And don't you want to know what she does?" Sten asked, almost pleading.

"She doesn't know anything," Crittondone lowered his sword. "She can't even speak. She's just trying to trap you, huntsman."

"She knows what's happening here. We need her. Let me help her. She can have my food if that's what it takes."

"Fine huntsman, but we tie her up. We can't have crazy running amok in our camp. Bind her hands and feet." Two soldiers came forward with rope.

THREE SOLDIERS WORKED at driving the stake into the earth. The thing must have been five feet long. How strong did they think she was?

After about twenty minutes, there was little more than six inches above the ground. They looped one end of the rope, tied to her feet and ankles, around the shaft of the stake and then pulled it up through a ring in the top. When they had finished she could barely stand and was forced to crouch near the stake.

"I'm sorry," said Sten. He couldn't look her in the eye. Her eyes were still darting around the tent. Every time she closed them, she screamed and shook as though she was waking from a nightmare.

"I'm so sorry." He walked over to her and placed his hands on her shoulders. "Try to get some sleep. You're safe here."

She shook her head so violently that she almost fell over onto the stake. Sten returned to his cot and pulled his damp blanket up over his cold body. It felt good on his sore body, the little bit of warmth the blanket gave.

He closed his eyes letting the sound of the rain, ease his mind into sleep.

The sleep however, did not last very long, sounds from outside of the tent woke him, and he was up in an instant. Cries echoed in the dark beyond the tent. What was it now? Had the Hoppers come for their quarry?

He rushed from the tent, rainwater spattering him as he brushed back the door. Soldiers were running to and fro, some gathering torches, others arrows. The rest had steel drawn. All looked ready for a fight.

"What is it?" Sten asked of the nearest soldier.

"Hoppers, whole big mess of 'em. Looks like they've come to finish us this time. Seems like they're comin' from everywhere." The soldier ran off. Sten glanced around trying to find something with which he might arm himself. He only found a spear. A weapon to which he had never been particularly partial. His had been a bow, but he couldn't seem to find one that wasn't in the hand of a soldier. He took the spear, it would have to do.

He followed the flow of soldiers that seemed to be heading to the outside of the camp. *It must be where the Hoppers are coming from.*

The soldiers were at the ready, waiting, the last few stragglers coming into place. Crittondone stood at their center, the deep baritone of his voice barking out orders. His long sword held aloft in one hand. He may have been a surly old cur, but he was a good leader, Sten had to give him that.

The great horde of Hoppers sat on their haunches waiting, a sea of eyes glowing in the torch light. Silence pervaded the camp. But the faces of the two thousand or so men that remained of the Queen of White Lilies northern expeditionary force stood, resolute in the face of their foe. Anger dictated their resolve. Finally, they would have a chance at a fair fight.

"Warm blood! Warm blood! Tell Queen of great feast, gave us. When meet warm blood queen soon! Tell her their new king! One-eyed King of cold blood!"

"Come on then, you great brute! Let's see what you can do when we aren't sleeping. Set your flesh against our southern steel, and we'll see which is stronger!" Commander Crittondone shouted back at the great Hopper Durdar.

A great cry rose from the ranks of the southern soldiers of the White Lily. And even as their voices still echoed in the night a chorus went up from the Hoppers.

Gitcha, Gitcha, Gitcha-a-Laroooooooooo!

Gitcha-Yit-Sonn-Gahrd, Gitcha-Yit-Sonn-Gahrd!

"Send message to Queen Lily, coming south, claim what ours! Get cold cousin killers!"

Slit trenches and pointed stakes separated them, but the horde came on anyway.

Sten watched in silence as the men cried in response to the horde before them. Razor steel that shone in the yellow light of the torches, raised in challenge to the great horde, defiant, resolute, hungry.

Arrows whistled above his head, and there was a horrid gargling cry as some found their mark in the night.

The arrows were met with a salvo of poison darts and even a few needle spears thrown with wild disregard.

They didn't they seem to be able to use them very well. A gift from their southern cousins? Maybe. But more likely it was this Lord of Green Boughs. The southern Hoppers had been given and instructed how to use the weapons by men hundreds of years before, but their northern cousins had weapons of their own. Long sharp claws that the southern breed did not have.

The spears were long with a razor's end, barbed, so that it couldn't be pulled out once buried deep inside flesh or armor. A spear whizzed past his head, and he ducked, waiting for the next.

He heard a scream from behind him. He turned and ran toward his tent where Kritcha was still tethered to the stake in the ground.

"Stenwith!" the shout came from behind Sten in the direction of the battle. "Go and get your Faytall; bring her out for these lousy louts!"

Sten kept going toward the tent.

A cry went up from the soldiers of the White Lily, and Sten ducked inside the tent spear in hand.

Her eyes were crazed, darting around the dimly lit

interior of the tent. He ran over to her and grabbed her by the shoulders. She screamed again piercing and high, Sten winced.

He didn't notice the flap to the tent opening behind him. It was the stench of swamp that brought him to attention. Before he could turn around, a webbed fist bludgeoned the side of his head.

He fell to the side and rolled, springing back on to his feet. A little dizzy but ready to fight the Hopper. He still held the spear, but they were so close could he even get the point down if it rushed him.

As if to answer his question the creature lunged, and he tried to bring the spear down in time but it was too late. The brute had him.

Razor teeth and sharp claws bit into him. Old wounds were torn open as they rolled on the floor. More of the brutes poured in from all sides. Kritcha let out more blood-curdling screams. They had her up and were sawing at her tethers with their long claws. They had her free! Sten struggled against the Hopper that held him down. Two Hoppers vanished beyond the wall of the tent. He had to get to her.

The last Hopper grinned down at Sten.

"Great hunter of south. Not so great, not so strong." It hissed at Sten, licking its teeth. "Warm blood, fine feast, warm skin, fine cloak."

The grin turned into an open-mouthed smile, and the thing leaned in. Sten swung his head up, catching the beast full in the face. The razor teeth cut his head, but for the moment the creature was taken aback. Sten knew it was his only chance.

Grabbing the spear, he swung it, catching the Hopper with the shaft. It howled out:

Gitcha, Gitcha, Gitcha!

Sten swung again knocking the creature over his cot and out of the tent. He hurried to follow it outside. The fight wasn't over yet. It sat poised to leap, bulbous black eyes illuminated in the torch light. Sten pointed the spear, and it hissed, hopping back toward the outside of the camp.

He made to chase it, but a scream brought the thought to a halt. Kritcha! He needed to find her and fast, if they got away with her he would never know what was going on up in this forest.

Following the cries he recognized as Kritcha's, he drew near to where the fighting had been the heaviest. Men limped past, darts and needle spears protruding from their armor. A fog-like stench hung in the air, so heavy Sten could taste it. The rain had stopped, and the smell of blood mingled with fear, and swamp pervaded his very being.

His bare feet sunk into the thick mud that coated the ground. He stepped on bodies, both men and Hopper. He had to find her. He kept going forward.

"Come on, you lousy frogs! If you want her so bad, then come and get her!" Crittondone shouted above the din of the receding battle.

"Great cowards! One-eyed coward! Come and take the Faytall, come on then and show us your mettle!"

There was nothing. It was eerie that silence. No man shouted, no Hopper called. There was only the sound of his own breath in the night. The battle was won. The Hoppers gone. For now.

"That's twice I've found your Faytall, *huntsman*, I don't think there'll be a third, else I'll kill her myself and save us the trouble."

Crittondone waved two soldiers over and nodded to Kritcha, "Tie her up good and tight, I don't want her running around our camp." His voice sounded tired. He turned and started to walk away, but Sten stopped him.

"Why did you save her?" he asked the gruff old commander, who looked over his shoulder at him.

"I didn't save her. I was defending my camp and my men. They wanted her, and they had to kill me to get her. I guess they didn't think they could best me. I saved my men and my camp. Not her." Crittondone turned and walked away, his head held high. Unbent, tall, and proud. Commander of the White Lily.

CHAPTER SEVENTEEN

S ten sat up. Outside in the twilit dawn he heard the soldiers working to break the camp. Everything was wet, soaked through by the night's rain. A chill ran down his body, and he realized that he was still wearing the wet trousers and shirt he had found in his haste the night before.

He looked at where the woman lay, still sleeping. Curled into a tight ball around the stake they had tied her to. Her hair was a matted tangle of blood and sticks and leaves. Her clothes a tatter of soiled rags.

Sten hobbled over to her and knelt down over her. She was shivering. He should have given her the blanket. Too late for that now though. He clasped his hand around her shoulder, shaking her gently to wake her up.

"Kritcha," he whispered in her ear.

She jumped, and he pulled back from her.

"Where?" she started, but Sten stopped her.

"You're safe for now," he said, looking at her battered body.

"Who are you? Where am I?" she asked straightening out, stretching out the stiffness from sleeping on the ground.

"I am Stenwith Harrison, and this is the camp of the northern expeditionary force of the Queen of White Lilies."

"How did I get—" she stopped and stared at Sten. A wave of realization washed over her face.

"You're the one," she sat up, excitement growing on her battered face. "The one from the forest palace. The one who couldn't talk." Sten unconsciously rubbed his neck; it still hurt, but at least he could talk and eat now. "You made it out alive. The big Laroo didn't make a cloak of you then?

"No, I didn't give him the chance." Sten looked at the tent flap almost expectantly. "They found you in the woods," he looked back at her. "You were mumbling and walking around in circles. Do you remember anything?"

She looked at him, her eyes distant as though she was seeing the other side of a great chasm.

"You went through the wall. You and the big one," her eyes focused on him. "I came after, into the freezing water. I found one of them, one of the others and Green Boughs..." her eyes lost their focus again.

"What about the others? The other soldiers I mean.

Did you see them? Were they with you?" he asked, moving slightly closer.

She shook her head slowly.

"Three arms." she said, her eyes still fixed in the distance.

"What?" Sten asked, confused.

"He had three arms..."

"Who did?"

"Green Boughs." Her eyes moved back to Sten. They fixed there on his own. Dark green and cold. What he saw there chilled him even more than damp morning air. There was pain and sorrow beyond what anyone ought to have. And a calm, quiet strength that most men would have shied away from, but Sten couldn't look away. His eyes were fixed upon hers, which begged him without ever saying a word, for something he knew he couldn't give her.

Without breaking his gaze, he asked,

"What do mean? Three arms?"

"He had three arms." Her voice was slow, as though she was speaking to a child. "He wanted our mother or some mother at least. He wanted the waters' hold to attack south, something about your queen."

Sten rocked back on his heels moving away from her.

"What will you do? What will she do, this Queen of White Lilies?"

"I'll tell her all of this." Sten turned to the flap. He hung his head. "She will want to see you, but they won't let you come. They're going to leave you tied here."

"What?!" Panic rose in her voice. "They'll find me. That big Laroo wants my eyes and Green Boughs my life. They already tried once again last night. No! You can't leave me here like this!" She pulled at her ropes, shaking her head violently.

"I know, but they're scared of you; they think you're a Faytall."

"A what?" she asked, examining her ropes.

"A Faytall. Women of legend. A woman that comes in the night and drains the life from men, catching them in a trap only to show them their folly when it is already too late."

"And they'll leave me to die? Because of a myth?" She tugged at the ropes again.

"That and they think you're crazy." He sighed and turned back to face her. "I want to help you, but I'm sorry." He shook his head.

Sten stood up. The flap to the entrance burst open.

"Still seduced by the Faytall, eh, huntsman?"

"No, I was just—" Crittondone cut him off.

"It doesn't matter, huntsman. Your tent is the last to come down; gather your things, we're leaving." Crittondone looked at Kritcha.

"She is almost pretty. I would have thought you could have dreamed better for your Fay-tall, huntsman."

"Can't we at least give her a blanket?" Sten asked.

Crittondone turned toward him.

"If you don't want one, then by all means." Crittondone left the tent.

Sten moved to his cot. He bundled up his blanket and dropped it down in front of her.

"That's it? That's all your effort?"

Sten sighed. He looked down. Avoiding meeting those deep green eyes.

"She'll send me back. There are too many questions that still need to be answered. Like this Green Boughs. What does he want in the south?"

"You might have a difficult time asking him."

Sten looked up at her. His caution gone.

"Why would I?" he asked.

"I might have cut off his third arm and kicked him off a cliff. Unless you can raise the dead." She picked up the blanket.

"I don't trust a death I don't see."

He heard the soldiers pulling up stakes outside the tent.

"Will you wait to hold my body until it is cold and lifeless?" She held up the blanket. "Will you watch the light fade for yourself?"

"No. I won't watch that light fade," he turned toward the entrance. "Not yet."

He left the tent just as the soldiers outside let the ropes that anchored it fall. He still didn't have boots on.

CHAPTER EIGHTEEN

K ritcha sat motionless. The tent fell over her, covering her in darkness that in a moment was gone, as the soldiers rolled the canvas tent. Taking great care to avoid the rabid northern Faytall. All the while she held the blanket, little help though it was.

She sat and watched as the last of the camp was disassembled and packed away. She was still holding the blanket when the last column of men disappeared. She set it down in the mud. Pulling at the ropes she tested their strength and the strength of the knots again. She tried to wiggle the stake. Nothing. It must have been driven in three or four feet. Even the rain didn't loosen it. She sighed, closing her eyes.

Kritcha shook violently on the ropes. Screaming out her frustration until her throat burned and her wrists and ankles were bloodied from the effort.

She threw herself back down, hopeless, into the mud. She rolled over, squelching in the mud as she did. It covered her head to toe; she really must look a fright now, no wonder they had thought her crazy.

Something caught her attention. Something metallic half wrapped in the blanket. Kritcha sat up, pulling the blanket closer through the mud. Out of its folds the object emerged. It was long and silver. A small dagger. Maybe he did care? Maybe he did want to help? She hurried, desperate to be free, hacking and slicing the rope that held her.

When at last she had removed all the rope she stood, a little dizzy, but free at last. She glanced around. There was nothing in sight, only the remnants of the southerners' camp. Wooden stakes driven in the ground to keep enemies at bay. Trenches to slow them further and to shit into. She jumped over one such trench narrowly keeping from sliding back down into the foul sludge at the bottom.

When she made it to the trees she took to the branches moving quickly. Moving silently, like only she knew how. She didn't know how long it would take her to get there, but that didn't matter. She had business she needed to attend to. So, she went north, in a direction she knew.

KRITCHA STOOD at the edge of the village. It was quiet.

There were no voices, no sounds of children playing, no men or women working. The houses were black. Charred to ash from the fires of the Laroo. She walked slowly forward. Tasting the blackened earth with each painful step. Listening to the sounds of the forest. Birds and squirrels that paid no mind to the plight of the village. And why should they, she thought. Why should anyone? It wasn't their loss. It was only hers.

She found the bones. Exactly as the soldiers had left them. Neat piles. Twenty-five of them with as much of the bodies as the soldiers could find. Some were only skulls. Some she could hold in the palm of her hand. She thought of whose it had been. There had been so many new little ones the last time she had come she hadn't even learned their names.

Tears ran down her cheeks. She sat on her knees cupping the skull in her hands. Hoping that maybe she could give it more comfort now than it had known in its last moments of life. She looked around at all the rest. What comfort could she give them now? What guidance? They were alone. Alone to reach ancient gray shores. Alone to find peace.

It took her hours to dig the first grave. There were times when she couldn't work anymore, and she would just have to stop and cry. Sometimes it would be a few minutes or what seemed like hours before she could pick up the shovel and start again. After the first it became easier. Emotionally if not physically. Her hands blistered and her back ached. Her arms throbbed, but she kept going. She had to give them peace.

It took her five days to dig them all. When she was done her hands were bleeding, and she was covered from head to toe in mud and ash. She placed a little monument above each grave. They were simple. A lone stick, dead, not cut from a living tree. Upon each she carved the symbol of the five sister moons and the name Vitger for what they had called their little village. She gave names to only two of the markers, one for her friend and teacher, Calleh. And the other for his wife, Semila. They were that last she buried and they were by far the hardest.

With her work done she walked half asleep to the edge of the small lake where the village sat. She sat on a rock letting her feet dangle in the cool water. Her feet drank in the cool flavor of the water. It tasted refreshing after so much death and the bitter tang of ash. A warm breeze blew against her face, rustling her matted hair, which hardly moved, thick with mud and sweat. She closed her eyes, and she could still see the light of three sisters through them.

She could smell them. The rotten stench of swamp. She heard the crackle of the flames as her friends were consumed by them. Now she would have new night-mares to add to those that had tormented her for so long. New faces to watch contorted in pain and terror. New screams to add to her own in the night.

Kritcha sat for a moment taking long, slow breaths.

She listened to the sounds of life all about her. The crickets that chortled ceaselessly. The ambling of a raccoon come for a drink. The mosquitoes that flitted about her, invisible in the dark, humming out their sanguine-filled desires.

They didn't care for the dead. They did not miss the dead. Only she would miss. Only she would care.

Kritcha opened her eyes. She watched the light of three sisters upon the smooth surface of the lake. Who was her mother? What could she have been to draw such sinister attentions? She wondered if it would stop or if more would come for her.

There was a sound of soft mud squished under foot. She turned to look. The raccoon had gone. Ripples danced across the surface of the lake. She closed her eyes and took one more deep breath. They had come again.

ACKNOWLEDGMENTS

I would like to extend the sincerest and most heartfelt thank you to all those that helped me to make this, my first published work, a reality. To my fiancé Megan Leavy for pushing me through all the self-doubt. And to Joe and Elaine, my parents, for being the very first readers, no matter how terrible it was then.
To the quality department at RLM, especially Jesse Lundy and Troy Bivens.
And to my editor, Erica Orloff, without whom this book would be a shamble.
To Boyd Craven who gave me all the advice he could and all that I would take on self publishing.
Last but certainly not least, to you the reader, for taking the risk and sharing the adventure. I hope you will come back for many more.
Thank You.

ABOUT THE AUTHOR

Michael Asselin was born and raised in Michigan and has lived there his entire life. Spending most of his summers in Michigan's upper peninsula he fell in love with the woods-filled north and reading fantasy stories. It was up there on one of those magical summers where he first tried his hand at writing with a typewriter bought at a garage sale. He has been working at the craft ever since.

Made in the USA
Monee, IL
11 January 2020